Summon All Heroes

A Novel

By

Edgar John L'Heureux

Sabal Palm Press

Edgar J. L'Heureux, Jr.
Post Office Box 756
Goldenrod, Florida 32733

ACKNOWLEDGEMENT

Special recognition for Mary Ann McGee of Oviedo, Florida, a wonderful person. I salute her care, thoughtfulness, and the encouragement she offered as I was writing this novel.

Special thanks once again to my great friend Laura Noveck of Wordmasters, Leesburg, Florida, for her skillful assistance in making this novel best presentable to the reader. Well over twenty years, Laura and I have worked harmoniously together. Her genuine concern and thoughtful suggestions have helped bring this novel to reality.

Grateful cover photography credits are extended to my good friend, Joel Horrell of Longwood, Florida.

This book is dedicated to . . .

All those marvelous people who purchase my books, who enjoy my work, and who take the time to comment favorably on my writing efforts. Their heartfelt kindness eases the burden and firms the step along the lonely and difficult path for the hopeful writer.

*"Words are things; and a small
Drop of ink,
Falling like dew upon a
Thought, producing that which
Makes thousands, perhaps
Millions think."*

Lord Byron (1788-1824)
From *Don Juan*

*Everyone needs beauty as well as bread, places to play
in and pray in where nature may heal and cheer and
give strength to body and soul alike.*

John Muir

*When one tugs at a single thing in nature, he finds it
attached to the rest of the world.*

John Muir

Preface

Thank you for purchasing this fourth book in the Delbert Turner Collection. You are about to embark on a unique journey with the wonderful characters of the fictional Wahaweechee River basin located in Central Florida. This is the fourth book in a series chronicling the adventures of Delbert Turner, a reclusive Vietnam War Veteran, who has chosen to live in the remote marshes and forests of a large state conservation area. Delbert, along with his many friends, provides a unique experience of the Florida backcountry, its beauty, and its dangers. If this is your first journey with Delbert, you might want to experience his first adventure in my book entitled *The Morning of Joy* (2005) my second book, *The Cry of the Hawk* (2008) or my third book in this series, *Memory Evergreen* (2010). We are following Delbert into another adventure in this fourth book. I sincerely hope you enjoy Delbert Turner as much as many, many folks do.

Chapter I

"I'm tired, bone tired," moaned Duffy, the burly owner of one of the favorite working class eateries in eastern Seminole County. He locked both beefy arms as a brace atop his Formica counter and sighingly propped his food-stained work apron against the same. His worn chef's cap slumped down his forehead, as though it could fall off into a tray of clean silverware at any moment.

Wanly, he stared at his good friend, Dan Miller, sitting on a swivel stool across from him.

"You're tired?" accused Dan with a playful smirk. "How about me! I'm seven months older than you. I'm tired too, and, with more miles in age, I have more right than you to be tired.

"Maybe. You're May and I'm December."

"And, we're not saying what year, right?"

Dan arched his gray eyebrows, expecting agreement.

"Nah, I guess not, like a couple of old ladies guarding their precious youth."

"I don't mind telling, but I'm not going to post any flashy billboards or have some plane pull a banner across the sky at any beach."

Duffy chuckled, continuing to wipe his counter top with a damp cloth.

"We can safely tell folks that we have served our three score and ten years, and we are now limping through borrowed time."

Duffy donated another very brief laugh.

"Rough Monday, huh?" sympathized Dan.

"Typical Monday. Happy for the lull now before the lunch cavalry comes galloping in here. What time is it?"

Duffy had his paws in soap suds so often he had stopped wearing wristwatches years before.

"Ten twenty-two," supplied Dan, checking the plate-sized clock high on the wall behind Duffy.

"We must have served enough coffee this morning to fill one of those big oil tankers."

"Business that good? Can't knock it!"

"That part is great, but I'm getting too old for the grind. That hot kitchen back there this morning felt like all the global warming in the world rushed back there out of pure meanness."

"Cool outside. A gorgeous November."

"I know. I know. I hear it from the workmen every day."

Dan sat silently for several minutes, thoughtfully quiet with his hands around his second cup of coffee. Then he spoke slowly, almost softly.

"What are you going to do about it? Retire? Sell out? Or, one day lie down for a very long nap on that kitchen floor back there with eggs cooling all across the stoves?"

"Funny guy. Real funny. Is your business so bad you're moonlighting for some funeral home?"

Playfully he threatened to punch Dan in his face with his counter rag.

"No. No. Business is fine. But, really, what are your plans, old man? Do you have any?"

Duffy solemned an answer, leaning toward Dan as much as his ample girth would allow against his side of the counter.

"Not for publication. Nowhere. Swear!"

"Swear."

"I could never sell this place, too much a part of me. Burned too many fingers back there in kitchen hell to sell. Earned real spurs. A part of me. But, I think I have some relief coming. A plan that's forming."

"Oh, what's that?"

"Buster and Buddy," announced Duffy proudly.

"Your two boys. I saw them grow up in here for years. They even cooked in back, I'm sure."

"Even when they were young. They knew this business as good as me."

"You know, I continue to see them around on occasion," mused Dan. "What's their status?"

"Buster has a lawn care service. He calls it landscape engineering, fancied up, but it still means cutting grass much of the year in this Florida heat. Buddy is a master plumber with his own truck. Big outfit out of Sanford. He don't own the business, never wanted the headache with owning but he's got all the know-how, from unstopping sinks to replumbing big stuff."

"I've seen Buddy in his truck at a red light or two and I've seen Buster on the road pulling his big mowers on a trailer behind his van."

"Doing pretty good, both of them, but they're getting older, late thirties, and working outdoors in

5

Florida, day-in, day-out, is brutal. I swear this global warming is for real. Even now, warm for November."

"Yes, replied Dan. I'm afraid you are right. Even the staunch naysayers, many of them, are coming around to that way of thinking."

"When I said I needed help, they perked up."

"And, you are thinking they might make major moves in their lives and join you here. In the kitchen? Out front here? All that is required?"

"They might. Talks look great, going on right now."

"You do enough business here to support three families?"

"Yes, I think so. I've put a sharp pencil to it and my accountant has also. You might not know it, but I have been doing the IRA stuff for years. Maximum allowed."

"I'm not surprised," said Dan. "Smart move."

"You are one of my very best friends, I don't mind sharing some rough numbers with you."

"If you want. Your choice. They're safe with me. I forget easily."

"I know you're confidential on all of this."

"Without question."

"I've worked like a sled dog here for years. Built it up over the years. Twenty-eight years. We feed an average of four hundred people a day. Sometimes more. Mostly, a little less. The average check is only $8.43 per person, because of all the breakfast and lunch specials we run."

"To build a reputation like you have expertly done and to compete with the fast food giants."

"Exactly."

"And days open?"

"Say, you're up with me," exclaimed Duffy. "About 343. We don't fight major holidays. This is barbeque and cookout country, and our working guys

6

in their paneled trucks ain't around town on holidays. And only a few restaurants battle Thanksgiving, Christmas, even Easter. And, we close down two weeks in August just before school so I can recapture any of the sanity I have left. I have a little painting done then, fixing up little things. I skedaddle my carcass up to Alabama, spend time with folks from both sides of my family. What's left of both sides. Shucks, in one of the old houses, up Clanton way, on my departed mom's side there is still an overcoat hanging in a closet worn once by a Civil War officer who was a direct ancestor. I look in on it about every year. Smells like mothballs in that closet. Guess that's why it is still in one piece. Butternut and gray, looking like you could slip it right on for a real cold day."

Dan nodded politely throughout Duffy's proud report on family history. He had his ever present calculator in his hand, punching in numbers as Duffy spoke.

Glancing around, searching both sides of the swivel stool from where he sat, he found no one within earshot. Beckoning Duffy closer from the other side of the counter, he supplied an answer almost in a whisper.

"Your family business here with its fine name brings in about $1,156,000 a year."

"Oh, my God. That's so very close to the figure my accountant showed me. How do you do that?"

"You supplied the numbers. This little gadget did the easy rest."

"Say," said Duffy nervously, "that thing got memory? A computer?"

"No. No. Just an old calculator. See."

Dan clicked to a row of zeroes for Duffy to examine.

"All gone," he reassured.

"Good. Good."

7

"I do think it would work," summarized Dan. "Enough income with no mortgage and fixtures paid. Three families."

"That's gross, of course."

"Of course."

"Plenty of outgo."

"Of course, but you have always run a tight ship here. Well managed. You could be just fine if one essential thing takes place."

"What's that?" worried Duffy.

"Simple. Would Buster and Buddy get along under one roof and would they like the confinement here?"

"Wow! No wonder you run a big dynamite business. Explain more!"

"All good," he reassured.

"Good. Good."

"I do think it would work," summarized Dan. "Enough income with no mortgage and fixtures paid. Three families."

"That's gross, of course, as I mentioned."

"Of course."

"Plenty of outgo to be honest."

"As I mentioned, family business takes special care."

"They do, for sure. And, Buster, Buddy and I have talked a lot about just that fact."

"In the company of your accountant?"

"Yes."

"Good man."

Dan saluted with a thumbs-up.

"Have you got a family lawyer? A good one?"

"Yes. He's going to start sitting down with us next week. The five of us."

"A good lawyer, with business law as his specialty?"

"Yes."

8

"And the wives get along well? Their wives? Buster and Buddy."

"Two peas in a pod."

"Advice. Free. Not preaching, but important."

"Shoot. Keep firing."

"Get as much out in the open as you can about yourselves. Can't really communicate enough. Talk it all out, again and again. Discuss possible pitfalls. Who will do what. The spread of work load. Even look for crazy things to talk about. Beforehand. And document, document, document."

"Agreed. Agreed."

"I'm serious. Caring called serious talk to a very good friend."

Dan pushed back the patented Australian bush hat he wore everywhere, and stared at Duffy with determination fighting the birth of a smile across his sun-tanned face.

"Say, changing the subject a little, how about you and your company, old man, that *Real Florida Outdoors*? What's up in your future? About time for you to make some strong future plans too, I would think."

Dan smiled smugly.

"Golly Moses, what time is it? We're talking away. Blabbering on like there is nothing to do around here."

"Ten thirty-seven only," calmed Dan, glancing up again at the wall clock."

"Good. I've got until eleven ten at the latest before I have to go back there and check on whether I still have a kitchen ready for the lunch mob."

"The happy lunch mob you mean," corrected Dan.

"Of course. Of course," reddened Duffy.

"You really want to hear what's up with me?"

"Absolutely."

9

"Okay. I'll bounce some things off you, for a change, this morning."

"Agnes has me covered up here at the counter, so let's sneak around the side, where we sometimes go, a table near the side kitchen door, where those civic clubs meet. Quieter."

Seeing them move away from the counter, Agnes, Duffy's waitress-general with twenty-one years service, scooped up their coffee mugs in one hand, added a fresh pot of coffee from a cart to her other, and followed them to their new location.

"One more warm-up, Agnes," pled Dan, hands aloft in surrender mode, "then I'm done, done, done."

"Any breakfast? The usual?"

"No, ate at home and Mr. Important here has less than a half-hour left on his busy schedule for us to talk."

Agnes smiled and returned to the quiet booths and counter in front.

"I'll check on you, in case you change your mind," she trailed.

"What a whiz she is," complimented Dan.

"More than I could ever tell you. Valuable here beyond words."

"I can imagine. Pretty obvious."

"So, we got me squared away today, headed in the right direction. I'm excited. What about you, old geezer, seven months older and far wiser.

"Older, yes, but wiser? Can't claim that."

"You're too modest. What is the latest with Central Florida's Wild Kingdom? And, I'm not trying to cut you or be funny. Your *Real Florida Outdoors* is known everywhere. In the news. A topic of positive conversation a lot."

"Well, thanks. If you're right, any success we have certainly hasn't been for lack of trying. We've been after it, twenty-four years worth, after I left academia early."

"And, you have built a Central Florida empire with that new approach to ecotourism you invented yourself."

"I'm not sure I invented anything. We simply tried a new approach, opening up the wonders of natural Florida without having a zoo per se at any of our locations. That's all."

"That's all! C'mon."

"We have tried to entertain and educate folks with a variety of things. Movies. Slide presentations with Power Point. Lectures. Field trips. A bunch of things."

"Without a zoo at any of your locations?"

"Oh, we have live animals in temporary, safe carriers as color and emphasis for some presentations. Snakes in sturdy glass containers. Sometimes a raccoon, opossum, otter. Even a motherless bear cub and a young panther when available. But, there are great places for folks to see animals in Central Florida. A great zoo in Sanford and one over in Brevard County. Disney's Wild Kingdom too. We never wanted to compete with the big boys. Disney, Sea World, Gatorland. Too many folks went bankrupt that way. We chose to stay under their radar, take lessons from their expertise, and offer a slight variation to their mainstream allure by pursuing a repeat market they don't chase."

"Meaning exactly?"

"Now you are trying to pick the lock at our own little Fort Knox."

"Who would I tell! You're sworn to secrecy about my development here."

"Yes."

"I hope you know that I would extend the same."

"I do. I do."

Our plans in finding markets for what we do are pretty basic. Nothing mysterious, really. We don't mind getting crumbs sent our way from the huge international tourist market. We welcome it, but we don't chase that market. We don't find it advantageous particularly to be near the theme parks and the big crowds. We're too small of a fish in their pond."

"You're kind of a theme park!"

"If we are, we're narrow in scope. We don't offer something for everyone."

"Where are your locations and how many now? You keep growing."

"Eight in number. Several with us for years and years. A couple, fairly new. And, we are not infallible to mistakes. What business is? We've closed a couple too."

"Sanford is headquarters?"

"Right, Sanford. But, we have some rivals in activity. Deland is doing well. Titusville and Cocoa too. You might be surprised how many retirees live in Brevard County. Clermont has always been good, as close to Disney as we dare to be. Eustis seems well-positioned. Many retirees in Mt. Dora and Leesburg. Our location between New Smyrna Beach and Daytona is modestly successful considering competition from the beaches. Folks over there love going to the Ponce Inlet lighthouse. St. Cloud holds it own. All eight locations are on the outskirts of towns, started rural for effect, but civilization keeps creeping out to say 'Hello'."

'I don't hear the Orlando area mentioned?" probed Duffy.

"Orlando is a great city. But, what we do is ecotourism, in house with programs, and outside with travel trips and limited hiking. It seems to hold true,

12

subliminally perhaps, that the nearer we are to natural Florida, the more our intent and purpose resonates with our markets. Again, bright lights, congestion, tinsel town stuff are our enemies."

"I know your locations are rustic-looking. They look like 'old cracker' Florida. I've seen three, I think."

"Yes. We strive for that. Mood music, so to speak. We preach natural Florida and try to look the part."

"You mentioned limited hiking."

"Yes. We have several mini-busses that transport seniors to and from state parks having our favorite trails. We watch the heat very, very closely six months of the year and the distances we go just as carefully. We never go far. So strange, seniors seem to overlook short distances, and even call any short excursion a 'hike". And, they brag a little even when they are sometimes never out of sight of our bus."

"Really."

"Yes. It is psychological. They are out and about, outside amid nature, and the duration or distance doesn't seem to matter. Really head-scratching stuff."

"Makes your job with pleasing them somewhat easier!"

"You're right. The phenomena does often times. I was surprised years ago, but simply accept the fact now."

"Hm'm. There must be a reason!"

"So obvious, the answer is overlooked."

"How so?"

"Their bodies are suited for short hikes, or short walks would be a better term, and their minds comply, satisfactory accomplishments in their minds."

"You should have been a psychiatrist," deadpanned Duffy.

13

"Some people have accused me of needing to get my head examined. Yes," replied Dan dryly.

"Oh, brother."

"What's the time remaining?" asked Dan.

"Fifteen or twenty minutes before I get the panic call from yonder kitchen."

"Good. I'll wrap up about me. Nothing earth-shaking there. And then I'll bring you up to date on Mr. Central Florida himself."

"Delbert, of course!"

"Of course. Then, I'll scoot and let you feed the hungry masses."

"Fine."

"Basically, we concentrate on two things; one, having locations close to state parks with hiking trails, and secondly, being somewhat close to a number of retirement centers with each location so we can serve those markets as a kind of neighborhood history and nature center."

"Obvious when you think about it," donated Duffy.

"We are not averse at all to school field trips, club trips. We love any residue of travel tourists from the big boys. Gladly, we are happy with leftovers from the giant theme parks, but the worldwide tourist market is theirs to entertain. We know not to butt heads with their huge clout. They are the elephant in the room. We are mice, and we have to avoid getting stepped on."

"Probably smart. You have stayed in business for years with that strategy."

"Yes. Thankfully. Twenty-four years."

"So, what's in your future, old geezer? Like me, you're beginning to get a little long in the tooth. I've got somewhat of an exit strategy with Buster and Buddy. You?"

"I need a Jack Hanna!"

14

"Jack Hanna? Isn't he that zoo guy? Big zoos! And, television commercials and animal specials on television too?"

"Yes. That's him. You know he got his zoo start here locally in our very own Sanford many years ago."

"Wow, small world."

"I mean I need a Jack Hanna type. For my business future. Not he, himself."

"No, no. Of course."

"I don't have the luxury of your family carry forward. Buster and Buddy, I mean. You know, Lily and I have no children. We weren't graced with that good fortune. No heirs. No real family anywhere. Only my Aunt Marjorie, age 88, and our Maltese dog, Humphery, whom we consider a child."

"Yes," nodded Duffy.

"So, with ole father time lurking, I'm facing a complete shutdown later on or some kind of perpetuity with folks I've never known. Buyers! I love *Real Florida Outdoors* so much, part of me, my left arm, Lily is my right arm, because we have touched so very many people with our Florida showcase of history and backcountry nostalgia. I can't envision ever shutting it down cold. Can't abide that."

"Any game plan yet?"

"Forming. Forming. Like a picture puzzle in my mind. Getting clearer in recent months. An image I can almost see in the fog."

"Great. Can't wait to hear about it."

Duffy scooted his chair closer to their table, a reflex to brimming enthusiasm.

"I think I will see a consortium of several people as buyers. Good, passionate folks in their youth. Maybe late twenties. Graduate school types with degrees in zoology, botany, or history. Folks who also have a business climate leaning. Folks looking for a profitable career but also searching for a soul-warming career in helping and educating folks."

"Good grief, you don't want much, do you?" teased Duffy.

"They're not leaning on every lamp post in America, I admit. But, they do exist. I have time. I can look real good. I'll find successors like I envision."

Agnes stopped by their table as she promised, in her own expert manner, winning instant smiles but no coffee refresh requests. Dan placed a hand over his mug and shook his head side-to-side comically.

"How much time before the kitchen whistle? Filling up yet out front?" asked Duffy.

"You have maybe fifteen minutes. Lunch bunch drifting in, but slowly today."

"Right," saluted Duffy, "Admiral Agnes has spoken."

"Madam Admiral Agnes," she replied dryly with a faint smile.

"Yes. Yes. I stand corrected," laughed Duffy.

"Just enough time to take a break from the drama in our own lives, and pivot to the latest with someone more important, much more important, Delbert."

"Delbert, that 'king-of-the-woods" rascal, what is the latest with Mae Ella and him? His name is popping up more and more in the news even, in print, and in local conversations. Steadily up, up, up, in recent months. Began several years ago, didn't it?"

"Yes. And he hates the attention and notoriety. Hates it. You know how modest and private he is."

"Secretive, a better word, don't you think?"

"I guess that would be valid, but not secretive in any negative way. He just hates big attention, even very positive praise about his true worth in the world of nature."

"He and Mae Ella doing fine?"

"Finer than frog hair."

"How long they been married?   Seems like forever."

"Almost ten years. Hard to believe."

"Any really big news with him?"

"Big. Big. Gigantic!"

"Fire away."

Duffy looked suspiciously at the rear kitchen door but saw no familiar image through the portholed window that could beckon him back to work.

"Well, first of all, the current health update, like we always do about ourselves."

"Yes."

"Remember years ago, when the first topic was always how good business was going?"

"I do."

"And now any conversation lead is health, health, health."

"I suspect we are not alone on that."

"Do you think?" smirked Dan

"Yeah, I think. No brainer."

"Well, he's slowing down, finally."

"How old?"

"Seventy-one!"

"No way. He's in awesome shape."

"Yes. But Father Time has his way, you know. All that tough forest living for years, sleeping on the ground out in the open, living in that damp lean-to with the big tarp roof that often leaked is the kind of Spartan living that can eventually wear down a guy even as tough as Delbert."

"Clue me! In recent years, he has stayed with his wife, Mae Ella over near Oak Hill and Mims, right?"

"Of course. Much of the time."

17

"And, he has stayed overnight some in that small hurricane apartment intended for him in that great nature center named for him in the Wahaweechee State Park."

"Yes. More so in later years. At the understanding of Mae Ella, I night add, with she knowing full well his love for remoteness in nature."

"Hm'm. But still aging?"

"Yes. Don't we all. Arthritis! Bum knees and hips. Lower back. He has some issues, real issues. Walks with a slight limp now."

"So, what coming up for Delbert?" chanced Duffy, almost afraid to inquire.

"All good! All good!"

"Oh, he is giving up the old lean-to with the muchly patched tarpaulin, and he is going to sunset living like a homeless man deep in the woods. Reluctantly, he's giving into that. He knows its time."

"Smart."

"But great news for him in the next few months. Great news."

"He's discovered an ancient dinosaur species thought to be extinct for millions of years!"

"No. Get serious."

"Sorry."

"Three months from now, I will travel with him to Washington, where he and nineteen other self-made environmentalists from around our country, all with great special talents, will receive special recognition from the President himself in a Rose Garden Ceremony at the White House."

"Whoa! No joke?"

"He was nominated and easily had the credentials to warrant recognition like this."

"And, you were the nominating committee," sampled Duffy.

"Only partly. Many others as well."

18

"That is great news."

"More?"

"Yes. There is more after the lifetime honor at the Rose Garden at the White House. Delbert will be officially toasted for his long service here in Central Florida, at a big luncheon roast to be held at the nature center, his personal namesake nature center."

"Wow. When?"

"Next October, almost a year away. Cooler weather. Outside and inside there. It will be more of a toast, not a roast. What bad can be said about the man? Nothing, of course. A toast."

"He is leaving the woods for good?" asked Duffy, afraid of Dan's answer.

"Well, mostly. He needs to slow down. Have his medicines monitored. Eat regularly. Not keep long hours like he has done for years. Important things like that. He'll visit back. I'll see to that. I'll drive him around and he has an older car. He'll have communion time with his beloved Wahaweechee."

"And, he's on board with all these dramatic changes in his life and with the glitter part too? The President and big doings for him in March!"

"He's a little apprehensive meeting the President. The big toast will be a total surprise hopefully."

"Wow, I'll even close up here for a day if I have to, to be with everyone at the festivities."

"Don't close up that day. Have Buster and Buddy run things that day. He'll want you there for support alone. He'll need all his friends there to protect him from the media hounds. You know how shy he is and how much he hates attention."

"I do. I'll help shield him from any media rush and their cameras in his face too."

"Good. Date in October later."

"Oops, there's the signal from yonder kitchen. I'm wanted back there now. Got to scoot."

"Me too," agreed Dan, glancing at his watch, and finding the morning gone.

"Catch you soon, couple of days," trailed Duffy as he swung open the rear kitchen door.

"Count on it, as usual."

Chapter II

"How many of your birdhouses are going with us, honey," asked Mae Ella.

"Rekon, unlucky thirteen, near as I can count," answered Delbert, showing ten fingers on two work-chipped hands and then three more fingers from just one hand.

"Nothing unlucky about this craft show over in Lake County," assured Mae Ella. "You and I, honey, have been there the last seven years together, and just before we were married ten years ago. I showed my beads there for several years. A good place, nice crowds. Hopefully, we'll do some nice income this weekend."

"Always helps don't it," smiled Delbert. "Good folks at that craftin' show, downhome folks."

"Yes, always enjoyable, even years when sales were slow."

"You got some good-lookin' bracelets, necklace some, and them book marks made of beads that folks like. Purty colors, sparkle nice."

"A lot of work, many an hour, under my green eyeshade with my magnifying glass making me look like a miner in a coal mine," laughed Mae Ella.

"Work for sure," agreed Delbert.

"But, no complaints. I really enjoy it all, creating something, pleasing people a little, meeting new folks. And the extra income is nice too, isn't it, honey?"

"Darn tootin! And Dan pay me too when I helps a little with them critter talks around at them places where folks go. Plum nice too."

'It is, yes, and you often become the star of those events, I've been told and noticed that myself."

"Shucks, I ain't no star. But, I don't no longer get real nervous no more."

"Good. You are a huge asset for *Real Florida Outdoors*, and a huge asset for me with the craft shows, in addition, of course, to me loving you madly just because you are you."

"Sound good, for sure."

"Years ago, I struggled so much setting up my tent that I practically had to beg for help at craft shows setting up to even get ready for customers."

"Not no more," urged Delbert.

"No more is so right. I've got you, honey, a super whiz at setting up for the public."

"Our E-Z Up tent go up by its own self. I can get her up and staked down on all them corners in under five minutes."

"Yes, you can. A huge help. Huge! We're all getting older."

"Ache and pain come visitin' Ever' poor soul of us given time to come a knockin'."

22

Mae Ella nodded thoughtfully, and offered a brief smile of capitulation to support her agreement.

It was pitch dark on a very early Saturday morning, as Mae Ella and Delbert worked with the help of a bare sliver of moon, a porch light, and two flashlights, finishing the methodical packing of their Ford Econoline van, most of that chore completed the previous evening in daylight.

The days were getting shorter, the fall outdoor craft show season had begun anew after a blistering, vengeful summer that had roasted Central Florida into mid-October, making summer outdoor craft shows practically useless in attracting crowds subjected to oppressive heat and tempermental thunderstorms.

However, as the somewhat cooler months blessedly returned and, even through the usually mild and delicious winter months for which Central Florida was famous and the envy of Yankeeland, craft shows could be found everywhere each weekend within a hundred mile radius of Orlando. They were advertized well and attracted huge, loyal crowds. The aroma of enticing food and the waft of music throughout the craft parks quickened their beckoning allure and in decent economic times seemed to aid in the opening of wallets and pocketbooks, the hope always for the well-intentioned vendors.

"We should be all set. The big cooler, iced and packed, is always the last thing to go. And, it's in and you shored it up with the tables so it won't tip or hardly rattle. We should be fine. I've gone over our checklist twice."

Mae Ella ran her finger up and down her paper list and chewed her lip thoughtfully, in agreement to her findings.

"Sure 'nough, we's set. Let's get outa Dodge," exclaimed Delbert.

Mae Ella climbed the three small steps to the porch of their wooden trimmed with brick bungalow, their vintage 1934 modest but well-kept home that had been spruced with paint, nails, and masonry dozens of times throughout the decades, and opened their creaking front door to snap off the amber porch light, then she locked the front door with a familiar key selected from a jumble of metal and, by habit, shook the doorknob several times. Delbert helped her down the steps in the dark with two outstretched arms.

They weren't pulling their little Airstream trailer for an overnight sleep so early in the fall craft season. Rather, they would test sales success on this Saturday and decide later in the day whether to return on Sunday.

At 5:18 a.m., Delbert took the wheel of their faded-blue and spot-dented Ford Econoline and began their fifty-three mile journey west over blacktop secondary roads to Lake County. Traffic would be light on the narrow roads. Their expected arrival time of 6:30 a.m. would be perfect for an easy pre-arranged check-in at the show and the chore of setting up their tent and craft displays before removing their van to the vendor parking area by the 8:00 a.m. deadline, would be completed with ease.

Delbert, with his supreme concern for Mother Nature and her critters, always kept a watchful eye for roadkills when he drove the byways of Florida, despite the fact it grieved him so very much to see evidence of the carnage. He tabulated trends by location and the gruesome numbers, both figures always communicated to his best friend, Dan Miller, owner of *Real Florida Outdoors*, remembering vividly what Dan had once related to him.

Poignantly, Dan had said, "Roadkills, as much as we hate them, help to manage our roads better, as strange as that sounds. The counts and locations give us a hint to the wildlife vibrancy of an area. Not volumes of data but helpful hints. When little critters populate in numbers, that condition can mean that an umbrella species like the black bear survives as well there. We can campaign for lower speed limits in some places. We can campaign for the high cost of flashing warning lights on a limited basis. We can campaign for the erection of wildlife crossing signs, warning signs that highlight "Bear Crossing," "Panther Crossing," or "Deer Crossing." Things like that, all suggested, not etched in stone mind you, but indications from roadkill data give us something to go on, with this running battle of protecting wildlife with more and more automobiles and trucks on Florida roads as our population continues to surge."

Delbert had explained his reason for roadkill awareness to Mae Ella years before, citing Dan's savvy words, certainly not passed aloud to her in as eloquent a way as Dan had employed, but nevertheless, in his homespun manner the message had been delivered.

Mae Ella had enlisted herself as a vigilant helper on their motor trips around Central Florida, even keeping a pen and a small looseleaf notebook in the glove compartment of their Econoline to tabulate accurately their roadkill findings.

"There's an opossum," gloomed Delbert, their headlights piercing cones of light through waves of wispy autumn fog.

Delbert deliberately drove somewhat below the speed limit on backcountry Florida roads, sharpening and focusing his viewing success for monitoring wildlife roadkill. Moreover, practically everything he did in his waking life was geared to helping and improving the total ecological circumstance of his beloved Florida. And, his commitment over the decades in this regard had won for him the admiration of many, wide and wild adulation that made him

25

uneasy and even more shy than was his natural tendency toward shyness and modesty.

"We's gone twenty-six miles near halfway and we's done seen a mess of roadkill," groaned Delbert.

"Yes, we have," replied Mae Ella thoughtfully, patting her pepper-and-salt hair nervously.

"How bad?" chanced Delbert, glancing over to her silhouette accented in the dark by the Econoline's dash lights.

"Five."

"I think I know how dem breakdown. What dat notebook say, honey?"

Mae Ella knew the tally by heart, replying instantly.

"Two opossums, counting the one we just saw. Two armadillos, and a raccoon."

"My own count da same," nodded Delbert.

"Probably late driving bar folks, hitting those defenseless creatures, or fishermen leaving for the lakes, this being Saturday," sympathized Mae Ella.

"Too early in da year for hunters, 'less them bang-bang fellas out an around a-scoutin' up game doings with da season a-comin' up."

"It will start getting light pretty soon," said Mae Ella, anxious to change their conversation to a less gloomy subject.

Delbert remained thoughtfully silent for a time. Then he fumbled over his driverside visor, changing an ending country music CD for a gospel singing disc.

"Hope we do some good today," brightened Mae Ella, searching further for a pleasant topic.

"'spect we's will. You got some real purdy bead whatnots for them shoppin' folks."

"And your birdhouses are outshining my shiny jewelry," teased Mae Ella.

"Shucks, tain't so."

"Oh, yes it is."

"Tain't."

"Well, we shall see. Maybe the weather will be a good buddy and not drown us. The report last night for today was good. Sunny and almost cool."

"This here idear of fall weather a-comin' make a shopper shop some. After this burnt up summer we's done had."

"And with clear, cool weather, and the music drifting through the park plus the aroma of good food, we've got the stage set for the chance to have a decent cash register ringing day. Music and the smell of food puts folks in a good mood."

"Bring on dem folks. We's can relieve usuns of some inventory and relieve themuns of some wallet lettuce."

Mae Ella laughed aloud.

She loved Delbert's way of explaining things, never attempting throughout their marriage to ever correct his speech with a schoolmarm English lesson. Rather, she left alone his comical butchering of the spoken English word, allowing the Central Florida world around them to discover and enjoy his homespun uniqueness.

Mae Ella knew full well his difficult past, his father's alcoholism, his mother's early dementia, his need to drop out of school at age thirteen to provide for her, his ordeal of witnessing a family shooting, and, of course, his Vietnam medical trauma.

Saddened by her husband's scars of time, she always comforted him, choosing to applaud with all the others within his Central Florida galaxy of friends and admirers, his enduring good spirit, his positive attitude, and his appetite for purposeful, hard work, all laudable traits freely given in the stark face of such crushing lifelong adversity.

"Wild hog," pointed Delbert, slowing along their winding asphalt road, now somewhat lit with the faint pink glow of early morning."

"That makes eight dead critters this morning. God's creatures. Ugh!" lamented Mae Ella.

"That will hopefully be the extent of Mother Nature's funeral for today, we're no more than a mile or so from the show. Thank goodness."

Delbert nodded thoughtfully.

Mae Ella, now silent, looked wistfully out her window at the piney woods landscape that was surrendering to a smattering of small town commercial buildings.

"You knows that Dan pick up roadkill all he cans. Stops when he drivin' and get his short, square shovel outa da van and a-scoopup them dead critters, split guts and all. All he can get up wit dat shovel. Vulture feed on poor dead critters."

"I know. You've told me before."

"Nice doin's. Dan care 'bout ever'thin' wild."

"Yes, he does. A self-proclaimed wildlife janitor for Florida backroads," saluted Mae Ella.

"Yup, that ole' Dan."

"He doesn't stop in the middle of the interstates with cars zipping by at high speeds? You have been with him many times on those big, truck-filled racetracks. Those bad fires in our home county Brevard. Capturing that emu. Those ancient dugout canoes you protected up near Gainesville. Other times."

"Naw, he don't stop when traffic up and a-snarlin' wit speed but only he stop when safe and traffic down. Puts roadkill in a tight lid barrel he keep in dat *Real Florida Outdoors* van."

"What does he do with the remains later?"

"Plants them critters with a decent grave near back fence-line of his big place."

"*Le Terrier de Renard.* Not surprised."

"Some folk a-pickup paper trash, some beer cans and soda pop cans. Dan, he pick up dead critters. He carry a big drum of water too in da back of dat van. Sometime he splash water on roadkill spot, a tryin' to wash down blood stain."

"Unreal," donated Mae Ella, smiling and shaking her pretty head in disbelief.

"He don't miss a-gettin' duty done none, that ole' Dan. Him a real Florida guy, that sure 'nough true."

"No question, he is outstanding."

The park in Lake County, punctuated with huge, ancient oaks draped with lacy Spanish moss was bustling with crafter activity when Delbert and Mae Ella arrived to take their place in a short check-in line. Daylight had fully evicted night. Only a light, dewy mist remained that would soon succumb to the skybound orange-red ball that was sneaking glittering rays of bright persuasion through the fortress of majestic oaks.

They knew the check-in folks well from past years, and were beckoned into the park with waves and smiles. Delbert held their show documentation by his driverside window, winning instant nods from the familiar officialdom. Many tent fiefdoms of craft vendors arriving Friday evening, not Saturday morning, were already up and stocked neatly with crafts and curios, ready and eager for the passing crowds that would begin to trickle through the park in a little more than an hour.

Delbert drove straight to their tent location, marked on grassy ground by washable spray paint with a number that matched their show application. Their white tent was atop their tables and chairs in the

Econoline, its weight helping to muffle riding rattle, but, most importantly, it rested there to allow easy access so the tent could be set up first before unloading what would be arranged beneath it.

Mae Ella's delicate bead jewelry was sorted orderly in metal display suitcases and Delbert's handmade birdhouses were in sturdy boxes away from contact with the heavy tables and chairs.

Delbert had the E-Z Up white tent ready in a matter of seconds, sprung up deftly, like simply opening an umbrella. He was already hammering the four ground stakes in place through metal eyelets at each corner, as Mae Ella began to shuttle lighter items from the Econoline to the grass floor under their tent that now protected valuable crafts from the ogre of petulant weather.

In fifteen minutes, they were ready for commercial battle, really polite conversation beginning with folks drifting by their family business on neat display throughout their tent. Some in the crowd to form would become willing customers for Mae Ella's bright and shiny bead necklaces and bracelets, and others would select for purchase Delbert's sturdy and well-designed birdhouses. The day broke clear and cool, creating a perfect atmosphere for a craft show that would be accented by the aromatic waft of delicious food and the energizing effect of peppy, shoe-tapping, banjo and guitar music.

With their craft display neatly in place, tilted trays of shiny bead jewelry, accented by a purple velvet background for Mae Ella and Delbert's homemade birdhouses suspended by stout cords all about their walk-in tent, Mae Ella relaxed briefly at her main table and put on her green eyeshade and prominent magnifying glass, worn like a bulging eyepatch over one eye.

She had noticed over the years that prospective buyers at shows had high interest for crafters who looked as though they were actually working at their chosen craft. So, she always wore her eyeshade and prominent magnifying glass, and surrounded herself with her pliers, tweezers and other tools of her trade, placing them in plain view to encourage the viewing public. Often times their curious questions led directly to sales.

While Mae Ella readied herself quietly, hopeful for an avalanche of people soon to arrive in a buying mood, Delbert trotted off to one of the breakfast pavilions, carrying in his rough-worked hand discount tickets from their vendor packet. He purchased two cups of steaming coffee and Styrofoam dishes of biscuits and gravy. Returning to their tent, hurrying but not spilling, he found Mae Ella hungry and thankful for his breakfast surprise. Policing gravy from the corners of his mouth with his red bandana handkerchief, he trotted off again to park the Econoline for the day in the designated vendor parking lot.

Returning in his patented Delbert jiffy, he burst vocally with enthusiasm.

"Bring on dem good folks," he nearly shouted, smacking his strong hands together.

Rotating his leathery neck skyward, he examined with a smile a clear blue sky, completely devoid of clouds.

"Good day. Good day a-comin'," he fisted skyward.

"And the weather is an early hint of fall, on the cool side a little. Cooler weather is always a psychological plus," affirmed Mae Ella, as though she boasted a doctorate in human behavior.

A national anthem recording blasted with some static across an outdoor speaker, signaling the opening of the craft show. Everyone stood at attention with hands respectfully placed over their hearts. Then banjo and guitars played lively tunes at their makeshift bandstand, a forerunner of lengthy musical gigs that would be presented on a regular basis all through the day. The craft show was officially open to the public, when someone rang a bell at the little headquarters house.

A group of folks waiting patiently behind rope restraints hastened into the park when the ropes were dropped to the ground, a hurrying early surge of prospective buyers. But experienced crafters knew that the key to a successful show was a steady arrival of people all day long, coaxed along in a positive mood of mind, by the aroma of good food and the waft of lively, spirited music.

Craft sales were slow in the early morning. Folks stopped at their tent, festooned with orderly trays of gleaming bead jewelry and birdhouses hanging like lanterns. Many employed their usual dodge for early greenback commitment, saying, somewhat understandably, that they planned to scope out the entire show before making any purchases. The second most often offered dodge to buying crafts was the lame excuse that they would get something on their way out, not wanting to lug purchases around all day.

Mae Ella had been a crafter for many years, and hubby Delbert, now claimed a few years of experience himself. They both fully realized they would talk with a far greater number of folks than those who actually bought something. This circumstance was central to crafting. Staying genuinely polite and positive with everyone was the best advice. Both of them enjoyed this honest approach, realizing one had great difficulty in predicting when a good sale would occur.

They had heard all of the buyer remorse, but their smiles persisted always, respectful of expressed reluctance, even when some excuses were comical, bold-faced fibs. Folks were under no obligation to buy anything. In addition, many folks attending craft shows had no yen for bead jewelry, or birdhouses, whatsoever. They were there for a roaming good time, sampling good food and enjoying the bluegrass and country music.

However, there were buyers, on a steady increase as the day and the delightfully cool and clear Saturday morning moved along. Pendants, necklaces, bracelets, and earrings priced from as little as $3 to the staggering price of $45 began leaving their tent with regularity, stored away carefully in purses and shopping bags. Some new acquisitions found their way immediately to wrists, ear lobes, and around necks, gleeful additions to body adornment.

Delbert was also tallying nice greenbacks into modest wads of money in pockets of his faded khaki pants, making change often from a roll of small bills they brought to all craft shows. Nothing was worse at a show than having a buyer present a crisp $50 or $100 bill, and having no change to complete the sale.

His birdhouses were priced from $20 to $35, dependent on size, as their construction, fashioned by skill and bandsaw, and a handful of finish nails, was nearly the same for each. Approaching noon, Delbert had sold seven birdhouses, spaced sales that had sent him scurrying for bites from ham-and-cheese sandwiches they kept stored and hidden in their iced Igloo cooler at all their shows.

When Delbert had started to help Mae Ella at her craft shows, soon after they were married, he developed the habit of munching food throughout the days in plain view, while prospective customers paraded by their tent, many stopping to open-air window shop. Mae Ella had delicately coached him that it might be better to disguise eating at the rear of

33

the tent when high volume in foot traffic was slowing to peruse their wares at the front.

"Folks might get the impression we are on break or even lunch recess if we gobble food at our tables in front of them, honey," she had asserted in polite schoolmarm fashion.

Delbert, with his fine mind, deprived of much schooling early in life, but acute and sharp of mind nevertheless, complied with her bright suggestion immediately, retreating thereafter to the rear of the tent or even beyond, outside practically hidden from conspicuous view when he devoured her yummy sandwiches.

Mae Ella seldom interfered with his colorful, cheerful manner, as her husband was universally loved for his honesty, humility, energy, and enthusiasm, but she had coached him on one further possible business bombshell because she wanted so badly for his expertly crafted birdhouses to be a huge hit with the buying public.

Delbert had fallen into the habit of saying to possible customers, "Well, don'tcha know dem birdhouses am really squirrel houses dat dem birds use some."

"Probably true, honey," Mae Ella allowed. However, she coaxed him to alter his honest evaluation, saying to him, "You may, honey, give the impression that your birdhouses are not suitable for birds, only for aggressive squirrels when really birds are suited for them. Folks don't buy squirrel houses, but they do buy birdhouses. It's not your fault that squirrels are squirrels and sometimes invade birdhouses."

With his quick mind, quite able to process information for solutions, despite his lack of much formal education, he realized the error of his approach, and started to keep squirrels out of his discussions with

34

prospective customers, much to the smiling approval of Mae Ella.

By 1:30 p.m., they had sold $254 worth of glittering bead jewelry and pine-and-poplar birdhouses, a wonderful start to what was proving to be an outstanding craft show for them. Delbert stole away with a hasty-paced walk to the vendor parking lot and secreted their overage profit money in the glove compartment of the Econoline. He locked and then checked all four doors twice before hurrying back to their tent. Carrying loose bills around all day at shows was dangerous, greenbacks were lost easily, slipping out of pockets during commotion time with sales.

In addition, and undoubtedly worse for the business climate, was the haphazard practice of showing scads of small bills when making change on sales. The public associated wads of dollar bills floating around with too much success, a bad impression. The less money seen on transactions, the better, had become the finding of most vendors at craft shows. Never were they awash with money. Most of the folding green always sported the familiar face of a very early president by the name of George Washington.

The afternoon selling was brisk, not fantastic, but fairly steady, only a little behind the sparkling morning pace. Happily, the afternoon was punctuated by an off-chance visit at their tent by one of Delbert's old friends, someone he hadn't seen in several years. With the crowd just beginning to thin a trifle, this old acquaintance passed their tent, recognizing Delbert, then sitting at their front table, smiling at the parade of people, possible customers and devoted lookers alike.

"Land sakes, as I live and breathe, is that you, Delbert?" exclaimed Lois Spense.

"Delbert I be," he replied, recognizing her immediately from past years, volunteer work experience with Dan Miller on her behalf along the narrow headwaters of the Ocklawaha River.

"Honey, you remember Lois Spense, the nice river lady Dan and me done work for, over to the Ocklawaha," said Delbert, now standing to shake Lois' hand.

"You and Lily, botha wit us."

"Yes, of course. Remember well."

Mae Ella, still sitting at their table, smiled broadly up to Lois.

"Glad to see marriage is agreeing with you two so nicely. Wise choice, Mae Ella. And, I'll bet he feels the same about you. Delbert's a true legend throughout Central Florida and beyond. I witnessed his fantastic work firsthand when he, Dan and Lily Miller, and you too, Mae Ella, came over those three different times to dress up my narrow end of the Ocklawaha so the old river lady, my Miss Lois, could carry Yankee tourists up and down God's country without losing her bottom to a bunch of submerged deadfall in the river."

"I remember well," nodded Mae Ella. "Dan and Delbert did the work along with your hard-working crew. Lily and I were stupidvisers only."

"Stupidvisers! No way. You both kept everybody hydrated. You worked hard on the Miss Lois, moving things along. Food and ice so the men could get the heavy lifting done, work under and around the Miss Lois with stumps and branches in her way."

"If you say so, I'll take just a little credit," Mae Ella created a small space between her right thumb and forefinger.

"Everyone contributed, led the first time there by this unlikely hero standing here, Delbert. His

36

reputation for getting things done had preceded him and he certainly didn't disappoint."

"Aw, c'mon. Weren't much," scoffed Delbert in his familiar modest way.

"Delbert, sell me a birdhouse! Mae Ella, I don't need any bead jewelry. Hope you don't mind. I'd just lose it in the Ocklawaha, piloting my pontoon baby, the Miss Lois."

"No. No. Just fine. No worries. Let Delbert show you birdhouses."

Delbert escorted Lois around their tables and into the tent, showing her all the remaining birdhouses slightly swinging in place with the cool afternoon breeze nudging their stout cords, making them look like silent, stirring wind chimes. Mae Ella acknowledged the dwindling crowd sauntering by their tent. A few small sales remained, but the real worth of their success had come earlier, between 11:00 a.m. and 2:00 p.m., customary high foot travel times for craft shows.

Lois Spense bought two birdhouses, one for herself and one for her boyfriend, Ernest, who lived nearby her at the same mobile home complex. Delbert discounted both sales as a courtesy.

"Can I give Delbert a big hug before I leave?" laughed Lois to Mae Ella.

"Of course. But, he goes home with me," she added jokingly.

"No kidding. I couldn't feed him anyhow. I've seen how he can put away food when he's working."

Mae Ella nodded vigorously, continuing to smile.

Delbert and Mae Ella waved after Lois for fifty feet until she was out of sight, lost in a throng of folks leaving the show for home.

"We's 'bout done," deducted Delbert, "Crowd done a-leavin'."

"Yes, our day's about over."

"We's a-comin' back, honey, ain't we? Sunday! 'morrow?'"

"Sure, we did great."

"How much great all together?" pressed Delbert.

"Near as I can count, $478. Darned, darned decent."

'Darn tootin'. Sunday ain't usual as good as Saturday, but we's could do $700 for the weekend."

"All our dear animals will eat good and we'll have a little savings to put aside until the next show in three weeks. Very decent."

Mae Ella packed her bead jewelry in her metal cases. Delbert took down his remaining birdhouses and laid them carefully in cardboard boxes. Then, as the show officially closed with the loud rendition of one famous country monument, followed by a bullhorn blast, they pushed their tables and chairs toward the center of the tent and dropped and tied their side curtains. The show would supply security guards for the night, folks whom they had befriended before, so they felt confident about the safety of their tent and covered wares.

Although tired after a long day that began in the dark, they both had bounce in their step as they walked to the Econoline. Mae Ella carried a few personal items and Delbert lugged their big ice chest, that would get repacked that evening with snacks and soft drinks for Sunday.

"We's gots to remember them stack of dry towels. I heared them weather boys are a-callin' for fog and dew in da mornin'. Time right for it. Ourin tent will be sweatin' dew in the early mornin' when we gets back."

"I've already got a stack of good towels at home on the sofa. We'll put them in the Econoline this evening so we won't forget them," mothered Mae Ella.

CHAPTER III

"Looks like a fair-sized crowd tomorrow, sweetheart," glowed Dan, sitting comfortably at red sunset, next to his wife, Lily, on their spacious screened porch that ran around three sides of their rambling, upscale Cracker-style home.

Le Terrier de Renard, French for "Land of the Fox," was the name for their rural, seven-acre hideaway in northeast Seminole County, within a mile of the storied St. Johns River. Seeing a red fox dash across the property on the day years before, when they had finally decided to hock their future, working lives with the purchase of the choice acreage, encouraged Lily and Dan to thusly name their new, glorious patch of planet Earth.

Lofty pine trees were left untouched and protected, when they had their cracker-style Florida home built. Designing their long driveway to curve and wind leisurely between and around them, the path was carpeted naturally with fallen pine needles from narrow secondary road to their doorstep, a distance of nearly two hundred feet. Pine cones dropped in such charming profusion, Dan found himself loading an entire wheelbarrow every other Saturday some months of the year, just to keep their driveway clear, a chore he never tired of completing with happy spirits and a homey sense of accomplishment.

An acre pond postcarded the gorgeous vista behind their tin-roofed, cypress-and-pine abode. A menagerie of wildlife paraded entertainment most evenings of the year, their own private zoo, precious for nature lovers like themselves beyond any cost or charge. And, in early winter, a priceless time of year in Florida, now only a month away, flyway ducks from the North landed to sample their pond before heading further south on their annual migrating trek.

"You're doing a kind of Thanksgiving program for them, I believe you said," offered Lily, as she sipped her second and last cocktail of the evening.

"Yes, with Turkey Day less than two weeks away, we will be talking about Florida wild turkeys and feral hogs.

"Folks eat both turkey and ham too, at Thanksgiving, even though ham seems to be a more common choice on New Years Day and Easter."

"True, but we are doing both in one lecture as they match up well, same habitat, swampy marsh and deep woods. It has worked before, several times."

"And you expect upwards of a hundred folks, you said!"

"Yes, four minibuses from four different retirement centers and we'll have some other people too. Seems like we always do."

"*Real Florida Outdoors*, not affiliated anywhere special, has a great reputation everywhere," donated Lily. "At the university, I've heard it mentioned several times by people who have no idea I'm married to its founder and owner."

"Thanks, honey," beamed Dan, "nice words."

"Don't get too much of a big head," remarked Lily dryly. "You still leave the cap off the toothpaste and you don't hang up towels!"

Their mutual laughter awoke their Maltese dog sleeping within feet of their matching porch rockers. He bounded to their side, rubbing himself against their legs after fetching one of his squeaky plastic toys from his toy basket on the porch.

Dan tossed his toy the length of the back porch several times, left then right, then left again. Humphrey scooted and slipped across the pine-plank floor, cutely stumbling across a number of hand-crafted throw rugs as he retrieved and returned his toy to Dan for further tosses. Dan kept up playtime, knowing that Humphrey would stop all of a sudden during lengthy chase time, winded from his frenetic dashes. And, this happened, as always, suddenly after nearly a dozen feinted tosses. Humphrey flopped down on his favorite rug and resumed his nap, totally disinterested in additional running.

Lily and Dan smiled their silent devotion of love for Humphrey, watching him quickly settle down for sleep, before they resumed their conversation.

"And Delbert is on the program tomorrow again, right?"

"Of course. We practically can't proceed without him!"

"Makes sense to me, for sure."

"As you know, he's been adding color to lectures at *Real Florida Outdoors* for years. He's as comfortable now with speaking as wearing an old familiar sock."

"I remember when he wasn't," reminded Lily. "All that nervousness just being on stage, even when he wasn't asked to do practically anything, just stand there and look like a natural-born Florida Cracker."

43

"Yes, but he got the hang of it, over time, because we encouraged him honestly and patiently, and he always had support up on stage in case he ever got in trouble, tongue-tied, or, worse, enduring a rush of true stage fright."

"And now, much later?" ventured Lily, earnestly looking across to her husband, with her cocktail held quietly in her lap.

"A safety net is always there, some other proven speaker, a pro at his craft, always at his side in front of a crowd. Just in case."

"Good," agreed Lily. "Good! Delbert is too great a person and too valuable to everyone who becomes graced by his worth and presence to allow a misstep on stage that would disturb him to the point that his hauntings of Vietnam would return and shatter all his therapy progress and the huge strides he has made in recent years to enjoy life again."

"Exactly," said Dan emphatically. "We always put his best interests first and foremost."

"I never had a doubt, babe," awarded Lily.

"I know that," cooed Dan, stroking her nearest cheek.

"Delbert will do the color on both, I suppose, with someone else handling the anatomical and habitat information, all the heavy but necessary stuff?"

"Exactly, again."

"Who's the main character on this one, anyone I know?"

"Jim Marlowe, one of our regular speakers and one of the best," said Dan proudly.

"I know him. I've heard him speak. He's terrific!"

"Yes, more than once you've heard him on stage."

"He's the memorable kind," nodded Lily vigorously. "His voice is stentorian, kind of a cross

44

between a basso opera singer and a convincing, forceful politician. Really forceful."

"Stentorian," repeated Dan. "Wow. Named after a famous orator, some time back, named Stentor. Right?"

"You're a jack-of-all-trades, buster," credited Lily. "What a versatile guy. I knew I saw real potential in you years ago."

"Jees, thanks," clowned Dan.

Their cocktail laughter stirred Humphrey again. He stood up briefly but caved down into sleep mode again.

"Jim is one of our best presenters. He can hold an entire audience for an hour without slides, film, or power point of any kind. That's a real trick, but he can do it. Has many, many times. Takes pride in that ability. Most folks want to be entertained visually, a lazy way, but Jim keeps them awake, on the edge of their seats, he is so prepared."

"What's his history?"

"He taught at Florida State for years, biology, with emphasis on big class lectures and some field study too, in the wild. The best speakers at that level, big auditorium stuff with 200, even 300, students in attendance have to be 'live wires' or they get a buzz of ennui and boredom. The bigger the class, the easier it is to lose attention, as kids can daydream more easily hidden away in a big class far from the sound system and the presence of a professor."

"I know, I'm a university teaching gal, you know."

"Yes, of course."

"But Jim never let that happen during his college career. He controlled his classes and I heard words like 'spellbound' and 'captivating' from valid references when we hired him in retirement."

"And he and Delbert get along fine?"

45

"Two peas in a pod."

"And Delbert does impromptu color?"

"Exactly."

"And this high-powered prof works well with homespun Delbert and Delbert does well with him, not overwhelmed sharing the same stage?"

"Does extremely well. Isn't that amazing?"

"It is, really."

"Yes. But Delbert wins over everyone, you know how he is!"

"Yes. Disarming and totally honest, doing his own thing. Folks sense his total genuineness and unbridled enthusiasm for backcountry Florida, laughing with him as he brutalizes the English language as only he can do."

"Remember when we were kids, Abbott and Costello. It's something like that, not exactly but similar. Jim and Delbert."

"Yes. I remember."

"Poor comparison I guess, but it came to mind."

"So, you don't choreograph Delbert. No script for him."

"True. We tried a little of that early on, but we found that leaving him alone was much, much better."

"That makes sense. I would have guessed the same."

"We know he's not going to gross anybody out with any inappropriate remarks."

"That's a given!"

"So, all we make sure of is that he knows something about the subject. We would never dangle him out there in the cold on a subject in front of an audience where he would be clueless."

"Of course not."

"But beyond that, we let him go. His stories are so fresh and interesting, and his delivery so unique, almost always producing laughter and ease, we let him proceed on his own whenever the main speaker, in this case, Jim Marlowe, defers to him for color."

"And Jim is not jealous of the laughter Delbert wins from their audience?"

"Not one bit. He's the serious type anyhow, relishing his presentation of a detailed lecture, replete with facts and information he truly feels his audiences should know."

"Nifty. Everybody happy."

"Works well, extremely well. Thankfully."

Dan and Lily sat quietly for a time, absorbing the caress of evening, a twilight highlighted by bird activity across their pond, its shoreline only fifty yards away and clear of trees on the side near their back porch outpost. The wildlife picture show was a different, wonderful performance every time they relaxed for reflective conversation and binocular study.

They spent a good half-hour on their porch on winter evenings, pinched by early darkness, and often as much as an hour and a half during the shoulder months of torrid summer, the pleasant months of spring and fall. In stifling July and August, they usually sat indoors under air, but then they made sure they had two easy chairs scooted up to large, bay windows so they could enjoy the panorama of their fenceless zoo, also known to them as their "back three," a fond sobriquet they had bestowed to the delightful rear three acres at *Le Terrier de Renard*. One acre was pond; one, woodlot; and the third an open meadow.

Three nights a week, on average, they happily collapsed into easy chairs, away from busy, hectic days, Dan at one of his *Real Florida Outdoors* centers or doing field work in the remote Florida backcountry and Lily at the university acting out the drama of Humanities, either instructing in class with her department chair tenure or attending the somnolent drone of meetings that often seemed endless.

Dan and Lily treated themselves to cocktails on the back porch some evenings, but not always when they chose to relax, viewing their very own parade of nature. They sat with non-alcoholic refreshment often, iced tea, lemonade, bottled water, never wanting alcohol to become a habitual crutch for homebound relaxation.

Two of the four buses from the four invited retirement centers arrived at the *Real Florida Outdoors* main center near Sanford, Florida, at precisely the same moment, as though they had driven there in tandem. And, the other two buses soon followed, separated by only a matter of minutes.

Smiling hosts met all the buses, Dan himself among them, together with Mildred, his longtime secretary; and a number of enthusiastic employees borrowed from their company locations. Guests were extended a helping hand as they carefully stepped off buses. They mingled for a time outside, in the treat of cool November, chatting with each other, meeting new folks, and then they were ushered inside to the large meeting hall and encouraged to select a seat from a fanned array of well over a hundred metal Samsonite chairs arranged neatly in front of a slightly raised stage.

A lectern with an attached gooseneck microphone and sporting a Florida panther logo, black cases of audio and video equipment, two overstuffed chairs, a table holding an iced pitcher of water and two glasses, a partial view of a drop-ready movie screen were all in place at the ready. Two large and live plant arrangements in potted vases graced the eye near steps on either side of the curtained stage.

A long table draped with a linen tablecloth was present against a wall on one side of the meeting hall at all lectures. Platters of assorted cookies, urns of coffee, a sampling of two-liter soft drink bottles with buckets of cubed ice and ready Styrofoam cups would be hurried out from the small kitchen nearby during the question-and-answer session offered at the conclusion of this and every other lecture. Folks enjoyed visiting after lectures, refreshed by tasty goodies and pleasant conversation! *Real Florida Outdoors* made people feel special, endeavoring in many ways to ensure good, lasting memories in the minds of visiting guests.

Amid the low buzz of excited and expectant chatter that enveloped the modest auditorium, Dan strode from offstage to the lectern, beckoning for Jim and Delbert to follow him to their two overstuffed armchairs. The white and gray-haired seniors smirked and chortled politely when, as a collective group of ninety-seven, they saw immediately how Delbert was dressed. Dan smiled as well at their spontaneous ripple of amusement.

Speaking into the pre-tested microphone, Dan warmly welcomed everyone and then introduced their topic for the day, explaining that even though wild Florida turkeys and wild Florida hogs were not normally dining room table favorites for Thanksgiving Day, the time of year, late November, provided an excellent coincidental opportunity to celebrate the existence of these elusive Florida critters, biologically similar to those most associated with the holiday on the natural tree of life.

Then Dan half-turned at the lectern and nodded respectfully in the direction of studious Jim Marlowe and grinning Delbert Turner, doffing his quite familiar Australian bush hat as he honored their presence with generous comments.

"Jim Marlowe has happily graced our lecture auditorium at *Real Florida Outdoors* for several years. He is a true favorite with listening audiences everywhere. After a stellar career in academia here in Florida, he has been kind enough, now in retirement days from the university classroom, to honor us with his presence and vast knowledge of so many, many aspects of our beloved state. His lecturing repertoire is huge, having perhaps forgotten more about his topics than other experts in those areas ever knew."

The eager audience clapped enthusiastically as Dan extended an arm and open hand in Jim's direction.

"And, with Jim today, is another indisputable part of our programming itinerary here at *Real Florida Outdoors*, Delbert Turner!"

Applause broke out again across the sea of seated folks, now smiling and even laughing aloud as they continued to pound their hands together. Many in the audience had been treated before to the homespun Florida tales and side-splitting witticisms of a modern-day Will Rogers, Central Florida's own, the irrepressible Delbert Turner.

Showing his unruly mop of gray-black hair, Delbert, while he sat, took off his broad-brimmed straw hat, and waved it wildly above his head.

As the clamor for Delbert reluctantly subsided, Jim took Dan's place at the microphone, and added his welcome to the elaborate greeting already bestowed by Dan, who exited at stage left to allow the lecture focus to be directed only to Jim and Delbert. Jim began the body of his lecture with a strategic attempt to relax his captive audience.

"Folks, I'll spend half of my allotted time, three hours or so, on each of our topics today, the wild Florida turkey and then equal time on the wild Florida hog."

He paused for their reaction. It was instantaneous. Total silence.

"Just kidding," he added, smiling broadly.

That remark brought the laughter he had wished to win. He was a seasoned professional at public speaking and knew full well one of the cardinal rules of his trade, winning the attention of his audience early on by placing them in a relaxed, good mood as soon as possible. He piggy-backed on the laughter he had garnered.

"If I spoke anywhere near three hours on both topics, let alone one, I'd be talking to these four walls and tour buses in our parking lot would be long gone."

More laughter erupted. The audience had been won, now it was Jim's to lose as every good speaker knows quite well. Seldom, very seldom, did Jim lose the attention of an audience once they felt comfortable with him and they were eagerly anxious for his message.

"Let's begin folks with the Florida wild turkey, known as the Osceola, named in 1891 by a man named W.E.D. Scott, who honored the great Seminole chief Osceola with his choice of a name. You may remember Chief Osceola from history? He courageously led his people in the Second Seminole War in the 1830's, the most important war of three fought here against the Seminoles during a period from 1817 to 1858.

"The Osceola is found throughout the bottom two-thirds of Florida, but not in the panhandle. There resides the Eastern Wild Turkey, which calls home throughout the whole of the United States, east of the Mississippi River, with some habitat claimed west of the Mississippi River in Texas, Oklahoma, and Kansas. There are five other subspecies of wild turkey found throughout North America, but none of these have any habitat ties to Florida.

"The Rio Grande Wild Turkey is found in Texas as one might conclude from its name, but also in neighboring Oklahoma and Kansas. Merriam's Wild Turkey populates the Great Plains and some of our Rocky Mountain states, at lower than high mountain altitudes. Gould's Wild Turkey is found to a far lesser degree out west also, and there is a hybrid wild turkey found some in the Great Plains and Utah.

"The last subspecies, the Ocellated Turkey, sets up housekeeping in the Yucatan Peninsula in Mexico. Ocellated means its plumage displays eye-like markings. It is a colorful bird and quite striking with its eerie eye markings. It appears to look at you from many different angles, its markings resembling ever-watchful eyes. Spooky! This pattern of design is also found to be pronounced in some of the peacock group.

"But, as I've said, our Osceola is found only in Florida. It thrives in flat pine woods, oak and palmetto hammocks, and in swampy areas that are found in profusion throughout our state. It is a favorite of hunters, many of whom come here from far beyond our state border to claim this trophy prize. Its hunter challenge is compelling because it is so wary and elusive and basically, just plain difficult to find and track. Only about 100,000 turkeys are found in Florida. That may sound like a large number, but it really is not. All in all, it is accurate to state that the Osceola Turkey is a true prize for the patient and skillful hunter."

"Our Osceola is quite similar to the Eastern Wild Turkey, but there are some notable differences. Smaller in size and darker in overall color are most obvious. Also, there is less white veining in the wing quills, with black predominating the feather. And, when our Osceola folds its wings, the whitish triangular patterns. seen in the Eastern, do not appear. The feathers of our Florida turkey reveal more iridescent green and red, with less bronze color than the Eastern. Its colorations are ideal for its Florida habitats. The adult females, called hens, resemble the males, except they are duller and lighter colored. However, the female wing feathers are darker."

Jim paused and expelled a loud sigh..

"Confused yet?" he deadpanned.

A ripple of laughter and nodding heads in agreement, prompted a broad smile from Jim and his own chuckle into the microphone.

"I'll go on with the anatomical goodies a little longer and then you can 'boo' me when Delbert comes up and removes those quizzical frowns from your foreheads, as he does with everyone."

"We like you, too," shouted a senior citizen, seated near the stage.

"Well, thank you, sir. I appreciate that. Truly do."

"Darn tootin' we do," the senior added, before settling down.

Jim nodded appreciation a second time, and then continued his zoology lesson.

"The social organization of a turkey flock in Florida, as elsewhere, is determined by a pecking order of dominance. Males and females have different hierarchies and different pecking orders. Turkeys have home ranges, not territories, where space is defended within a given habitat. Instead, they quarrel and fight for dominance within a pecking order while sharing overlapping home ranges.

"Anyone snoring yet?" smirked Jim.

A laughter headcount by Jim judged that everyone was still awake.

"Do you want to hear about courtship?" asked Jim coyly.

"We all old 'nough," encouraged the senior who had blurted earlier that they liked Jim as well as Delbert.

"Yes, you are, by a few years," joked Jim.

"Many years," answered the thankfully polite heckler.

"Breeding behavior is usually activated by increasing day length in spring, but unusual warm or cold spells may speed up or slow down the process often, the love time begins while birds may still be in large winter flocks prior to separating into small groups as the weather warms.

"Courtship patterns include gobbling and strutting by the males. Let your imagination take over on what happens next."

Jim arched his eyebrows and practiced a look of shocking surprise. His audience was still with him, engrossed in his studious presentation of the Florida wild turkey.

"Hens are quite secretive when searching for a nest site. Prior to laying eggs, they may continue social activity with their flock, but their nest site is private. Nests are shallow depressions formed by scratching, and are usually in areas of quite dense understory; which still allows the hen a view, but gives sight protection from avian predators. Laying her clutch of 10-12 buffy eggs, spotted with brown, takes about two weeks. Usually the hen covers her eggs with leaves and twigs. Incubation takes 26-28 days, the hen sitting motionless and turning the eggs about once an hour.

"Still with me?" asked Jim with a mock shout.

"Yes," chorused the reply.

"Great! Let me tell you two more important things about turkeys and their young, and then I'll rest a few minutes before we speak about the wild Florida hog, and we'll get Delbert up here to tell some of his tales about old Osceola. I know you are anxious to hear from him and he's squirming over in that chair, just as anxious to get up here to this microphone."

Delbert grinned his infectious smile and nodded his head vigorously.

"Listen closely, if you choose, and have interest. I'm going to discuss briefly two terms about which you may not be familiar, but they both are so very interesting and show well the marvelous, mysterious wand of Mother Nature.

"The first one is called pipping. The poult, actually, the turkey to be in the egg, rotates within the shell of the egg, chipping a circle break around the large end of the egg, making a pipping sound as they work toward freedom. The hen, ever close, responds to the pipping sounds by making soft chucks, a form of communication that brings us to the second possible new term for many folks."

"Imprinting!

"Imprinting is a special approach to learning which is essential for the needful, rapid social development of the newborn poults into adults. It is a little weird, listen! Perhaps fascinating would be a better description. Imprinting takes place during the first 24 hours after hatching. The young poults learn to recognize their species, essential for survival. This clucking, purring, putting and alarm call period happens only at this time and cannot be reversed or done again."

"Day old poults quickly learn to respond to the mother hen's putt or signals; before leaving the nest and when alarmed, they freeze or run to hide beneath her. Slowly, the hen, clucking continuously leads her poults away from the nest. The poults form a brood group and start to peck away at food items, an imprinting skill taught by the mother hen.

"By the second day out from the nest, wild turkey poults are performing important feeding, movement, and grooming patterns. Within one week, they are regularly dusting with the hen. After two weeks, they are able to fly short distances and, by the third week, they are able to roost in low trees with the mother.

"Roosting is critical, absolutely critical, as it helps remove them from the real danger of ground predators. Roosting takes place about the same time that juvenile plumage begins and their diet changes from insects to a higher percentage of plant matter. Also, poult mortality begins to drop dramatically, coinciding with roosting. After roosting, six weeks, survival chances to adulthood increase substantially.

"At age fourteen weeks, male and female are distinguishable by plumage and body size. Pecking orders have formed, although the mother hen still dominates, until all her male offspring have left the basic brood grouping to create their own social units that are loosely formed at their early beginnings. By fall, about six months after birth, the full pecking order has been worked out and the young poults have a part in the social organization of their surrounding population. And, the early life cycle ends by winter, as the body growth of the juveniles ends when the flock separate by age and sex class."

Jim sagged audibly at the microphone, as though he had recited the Gettysburg Address and the entire United States Constitution.

"Whew," he exclaimed, "I need to get away from this microphone for a time and welcome Delbert Turner up here, I'm beginning to sound like some stuffy professor."

"Doing fine, doing fine," shouted up a senior cheerleader from the second row of chairs.

"Well, I appreciate that," acknowledged Jim, "but let's hear from Delbert now and some of his experiences with Florida wild turkeys.

Delbert, trim and fit, rose to his full six feet in height, and practically galloped to the lectern and its gooseneck microphone. Delbert looked the part of a Florida farmer this day, but he often changed his country and backwoods garb whenever he spoke. This day, he wore faded but clean bib overalls, a patched, red workshirt fresh off Mae Ella's ironing board, mudless work shoes, and a floppy straw hat that kept slipping around his head as he enthusiastically spoke. He plunged right into true and honest character, as if some imaginary spotlight had just beamed his way.

"Howdy, folks. Thanks for coming out this here day."

The audience, knowing firsthand about him or merely hearing positive things about him, were already chuckling with him, never at him.

"Yessiree, I had me some close up time with 'dem Florida turkeys. Close up 'nough to know them big birds ain't 'actly what you might call purdy. Ain't no Hollywood stars amongst dem male turkeys, for durn sure. Them males get dem beards hangin' offin da chest, a funny-lookin' growth offin da beak, a-called a snood, a bunch a wart-lookin' stuff a-called wattle or carnucle up on a ugly head all blue and red that look like a-changin' color like an old neon sign when dem males get riled up just natural-like or go to courtin' time."

Delbert took off his yellow straw hat, and wiped his forehead with an orange bandana he had stuffed away in a rear pocket. He wasn't trying to act like a modern-day Will Rogers, but what came across naturally was as funny and as unrehearsed as any hilarious onstage performance during the days and times of homespun Will Rogers.

"I knowt a story, all plum true, 'bout a young male turkey a-hangin' out wit a mess of peacocks. I seen it. I got me an ole woods buddy a-livin' in one of dem nice neighborhoods not fifteen miles from right here where we all sits. There a mess of good-lookin' peacocks a-livin' right in folks yards here in Seminole County, a-spendin' nights up in dem oak trees roostin' an' grubbin's round for seeds and like in da daytime. They just showed up from somewhere Lord knows where, and people done took up a-lookin' after 'em. Well, folks, this here good buddy tolt me a story whichin we seen together when he had me over ta his house one early evein' for a supper of his wife's good vittles. There amongst a flock of real purdy peacocks, mebbe 18-20 all tolt, was this here scrawny, young male wild turkey a-tryin' to be a part of dat peacock family group."

The spellbound audience swayed in their seats with peals of laughter and gasps of surprise.

"Dat there male didn't show no full plumage yet, bight color and such, but he darn-tootin' were a-chasin' dem young hens a-like he had sumptin on hisin mind. Them young hens was avoidin' him like da plague, runnin' under palmettos and a-hidin' out as besting dem could in weeds, in flower beds, in amongst dem oak trees, a-runnin' from dat male turkey whichin were a-doin' his level best to win some friends, even jes one. He weren't havin' no luck in findin' no friends, dem a-voidin' the likes of him likein him wasin a red-haired, harelip a-carryin' round a whole suitcase full of itchy fleas and a case of vomit breath to boot."

Folks were roaring with laughter, and Dan, hidden off stage, was rocking with glee too, his arms folded confidently across his chest while he reveled in Delbert's success.

"I cam back to hisin place again for supper 'bout a month later and dat scrawny turkey, still dare, had done lost some more weight, 'cause he was still a-chasin' after dem peacocks I rekon. Den, I heard 'about a month lader from my buddy, dat dat there skin-and-bone turkey jes up and dispeer one day. Rekon him jes fall down one day plum dead on da spot from so much a-runnin' and a-lookin' for even one friend. Never did heard what happen to dat turkey. Nobody know nottin', but ain't it kinda sad, ever' which way?"

The enthralled crowd commiserated with Delbert, unable to laugh only with the telling of the curious and perplexing turkey story, even though laughter had predominated their happy reaction until the mysterious end.

Delbert related other turkey tales and then invited questions from his well-captured subjects. He was barraged with questions, his audience mesmerized with his honest, folksy manner.

Jim, ever conscious of time and with an urging nod from Dan still hidden offstage, rose and whispered to Delbert words he often had used on previous occasions.

"Better cut off the questioning, pronto, we have this wild hog to cover yet, and time is moving fast."

Delbert lifted his brawny arms in a friendly protest to the crowd and sauntered back to his comfortable seat, waving a smiling thank-you. Jim thanked him profusely across the microphone, and Delbert received another thunderous ovation. Jim smiled through all of it, without feeling one speck of jealous rivalry.

The audience settled down quickly, as Jim began his wild Florida hog segment with his normal, expert proficiency, citing copious points and several facts with numbers on the life and times of the wild

Florida hog. He kept his word track very informative but plainly straightforward, as the lecture was progressing wonderfully and he didn't want to encourage any naps at their most successful juncture.

Delbert was at the microphone again at the conclusion of Jim's remarks, receiving gasps of wonder and suspense, as he related some if his own experiences of being stalked by a wild hog once for a half-mile, by a tusker he couldn't see, only hear, in deep palmettos along a narrow dirt road within sight of their magical St. Johns River. He had them all howling again when he related another cliff-edged happening.

"Oncet, I run across a trotting line of big boars and sows, mebbe six or seven, comin' at me jes across a real skimpy fence, closin' fast in ma direction." He had everyone roaring again when he said, "I was a-scoutin' 'round purdy durn fast for yonder limb to a-jump on and they's weren't none, noplace. Wooooeeee!!! A-sweatin' I was, likein to a big pig hisself I was, but it turn out okay. Them trottin' hogs came to trottin' more faster and a-squealin' likein da hogs dey was, until dey were plum gone da other way down dat dare fence line. Rekon dem was a-scared of me likein I twas of dem. Lordy me!"

The refreshment mixer after the most successful lecture was an especially chatty time for everyone. Folks milled around trying to meet and talk with Delbert and they extended courtesies and compliments to Jim as well. Dan was in the thick of the throng, munching cookies and sipping iced tea while he nodded and smiled continually, as though he were a candidate at some political rally.

The party didn't begin to disband until the four tour bus drivers stood in a loose line against a conspicuous wall, glancing at their wristwatches politely on purpose, until the subtle notion got breezed around the hall that regrettably, it was time to leave.

CHAPTER IV

"A turtle, right? A turtle! I've seen them all my life. I know what a turtle is. Lately, I've seen pictures of them in the newspaper a lot. They're in the local news."

Duffy was mildly annoyed with Dan, showing open palms and a quizzical stare, as the two great buddies sat at their favorite rear table in Duffy's popular diner during an off-peak food hour, an occurrence they often sought to catch each other up on east-central Florida news.

"Technically a turtle, yes," allowed Dan, drifting somewhat professorial.

"Whew, thanks a lot. I thought I was going buggy there for a minute."

"But tortoises are really a kind of subset, in lay terms of course, of the whole realm of turtles, which are reptiles, of course."

"Of course!" teased Duffy.

"There are mud and musk turtles, pond and marsh turtles, sea turtles, side-necked turtles, snapping turtles, soft-shelled turtles."

"Swell."

"Then, we have your typical garden variety type of a group of turtles known as terrapins," joked Dan, casting a smug smirk in Duffy's direction.

"Okay! Okay! Only because you're my good buddy, I'm listening to all of this and of course the main reason is my admiration for Delbert, whom you tell me is going to assist you as volunteers in relocating these turtles living in the path of the last part of the long overdue beltway to be built around greater Orlando."

"Tortoises! Gopher tortoises!" corrected Dan.

"Okay. Forgive me. I'm guilty again. Too many animal types beginning with the letter `T' for a dummy like me. Turtles! Terrapins! Tortoises!"

"You're not a dummy," said Dan.

"Well, thanks."

"You're welcome. Wanted you to know."

"Thanks again. Okay. Okay. Sanely and calmly, let me ask this."

Duffy boxed his hands into a neat cube.

"Assuming I don't, repeat, don't have to take a written exam prepared by you, the outcome of which depends on whether I keep my restaurant here or not, could you please explain, in simple terms, why these tortoise turtles have to be taken out of harm's way and how you guys and the so-called authorities plan to do this."

"Fair enough," shrugged Dan, allowing to pass without correction, Duffy's name assignment of tortoise turtles instead of gopher tortoise."

"Super."

"Simply put, it's the law. Gopher tortoises are protected. They can't just be bulldozed around like so much sand when humankind's development sprawls out to shake hands, so to speak, with their habitat. Conscientious, deliberate, and huge efforts and measures must be made to relocate them to similar topographical locations so they can continue to thrive in Florida as they have done for so very long."

"That's a great idea," blurted Duffy. "Something like human beings very aware of the little creatures in Mother Nature's realm and looking after their continued existence so that one day we don't look around and see only us, and only then finally realize, too late, that we can't survive either."

"Exactly. Nicely said. I better not hear you calling yourself a dummy again. If you do, I'll clout you on the noggin with one of your frypans back in your kitchen."

"Then I would be a dummy for sure, knocked wacky with a heavy frypan," laughed Duffy, enjoying Dan's compliment.

Waitress Agnes heard their laughter around the corner, and came by to say a quick hello, bringing with her a steaming coffee pot from the refill cart in the main dining area. She filled their mugs, wagging her head with a scold.

"Too much fun. Too much fun. You're having just too much fun."

Her banter sparked Dan and Duffy to howl again.

"I guess you're right, Agnes," called Dan, as she retreated from their table back to her duties. In a few moments, they settled down, and Dan stood atop his imaginary soapbox again.

"Remember when they got underway building some new rail stations when SunRail was finally voted as official, the huge transportation project planned for sixty-one miles of commuter rail from Deland to Poinciana south of Kissimmee? Not finished yet!"

"Vaguely," managed Duffy thoughtfully.

"Well, some new rail station projects were put on hold for a time and workers sent elsewhere because many, many gopher tortoises had dug inconvenient burrows, slant-fashion, into the side banks of the rail beds. Habitat! They lived there, easy pickings for burrows because the rail beds were build up with sloping sides."

"Halted progress?"

"Yes, postponed progress big time, until the gopher tortoises could be fetched out and relocated elsewhere."

"I've heard of eagle nests stopping construction. Even sometimes ospreys, I think," explored Duffy.

"Yes. Eagle nests mandated. The law. Osprey nests, mostly out of sympathy, and the good press it wins for development."

"But, I wasn't aware of any law by which these gopher tortoises are to be saved and totally spared."

"Now you know. Yes."

"So, how do they go about getting them out in the open so they can capture and relocate?"

"Very carefully."

"I bet."

"First, they survey thoroughly the gopher tortoise area to be altered by the advance of civilization, in this case the final beltway leg, a distance of a little over three miles. Doesn't sound like a huge distance, but when you are looking for gopher tortoise burrows, it is a slow and tedious process."

"No doubt," chimed Duffy.

"The survey is critical, and its swath, the places to be inspected and cleared is a pretty fair-sized area. Remember a vehicular road of this magnitude will be much wider, with all the driving lanes, than a railway bed."

66

"How do they actually do it?"

"As I said, very carefully. Kid gloves, so to speak. Has to be. The entire area has to be walked again and again, and probed, something like an advancing corps of rescue, police, and volunteer folks searching for a possible dead body when foul play is a possibility with a missing person case. They are looking primarily for active burrows, ones with tenants now, so to speak."

"You said probes! How so?"

"Well, something like giant probes that look and roam around inside the burrows, pliable, gooseneck types, like those looking down an esophagus of a human, only much longer and bigger, of course."

"They locate entrances and then go looking?"

"Yes."

"Can they tell the difference between the active burrow and one that is, well, kind of deserted?"

"Usually. Fresh tracks. Familiar litter. Scraps of food. You know gopher tortoises run hotels!"

Dan painted a mischievous smirk across his tanned face.

"Run hotels? What gives? Clue me, professor."

"Many other critters share these long, patiently dug burrows."

"Many others?"

"Yes. The Florida mouse. Snakes, like the beautiful iridescent Indigo."

"Shiny!"

"Yes, shiny. Iridescent. Beautiful snake."

"Truce," granted Duffy, holding up his hands.

"Other snakes too, " continued Dan. "Armadillos."

"Do they all fight when the rent comes due?" joked Duffy.

67

"Most of the squabbles come from neighboring gopher tortoises themselves. Mostly, they claim more than one burrow as home, and sometimes run into intruders coming and going."

"Trouble in paradise," sighed Duffy, sarcastically.

"Ain't it so. Ain't it so."

"Living things," shrugged Duffy.

"Back to search and rescue for them. Got time?"

"Slowest time of day, and slowest day of the week. You can proceed, if you still promise no exam."

"No exam. No worries."

"Good."

"It's really kind of high tech how they go about relocation. Some gopher tortoise entrances are obvious, of course, in plain view. Holes with half-moon tops with plenty of apron sand at the front. The size of the entrance is a strong indication of the size of the gopher tortoise tenant there. Naturally, the bigger the entrance, the bigger the user."

"Makes sense," nodded Duffy.

"The big adults are often close to a foot long and can weigh as much as 8-10 pounds. When the entrance is oval rather then with a half-moon top, it usually means an armadillo has taken up residency. These burrow dens can be large, some as deep as seven feet or so, and as long as forty feet or longer. And, to make matters more difficult, they have shorter side compartments where gopher tortoises often go."

"Wow, like Florida caverns or caves almost!"

"Well, something like that."

"They use a device called a burrow cam to probe for occupancy, to see if a burrow is active. It's a kind of scope that is somewhat pliable. It works fine, but it is not infallible. There are often these side tunnels as I have said and they present sharp turns

68

often, making them hard to explore. The authorities try to do everything they can do as delicately as possible before lumbering backhoes come on the scene to carefully excavate from the ground down."

"Makes sense. Safety first."

"Right."

"When they annoyingly, without bodily damage, disturb a gopher tortoise, this is exactly what they want to accomplish, having them move toward the entrance so they will exit and get caught in a so-called bucket trap."

"Bucket trap?"

"Nothing special, useful though. A normal five-gallon bucket that works well. Big enough, but not too big to maneuver easily."

"Okay, once caught, then what?"

"They must be moved within 72 hours to the recipient site."

"Recipient site?"

"Yes, the place where they are found, in harm's way for development or we wouldn't even be having this conversation, is called the donor site. The destination, within a hundred miles, to similar habitat and soil conditions, is referenced to as the recipient site."

"Pretty involved, isn't it?" gloomed Duffy.

"It is. The gopher tortoise boasts a virtual army of environmental watchdogs."

"No foolin'."

"There's more, but I'll wrap it up and let you get back to slinging that topnotch cuisine of yours."

"You mean hash."

"No, cuisine. Everything here is good. Real good."

"Gee, thanks. It's nice some folks say so."

"Just a couple more points and I'll shut up."

"Promise!" joked Duffy.

"Say, I just paid your chow house an honest compliment!"

"Just kidding. Go on, I'm learning a lot."

"By law, the gopher tortoises have to be moved to the recipient area, as I've said, within a hundred miles, within 72 hours of capture, to limit stress."

"They have stress, and don't even pay taxes."

"Funny man," joked Dan.

"Really!" he shot back.

"All creatures have some degree of stress, some creatures simple handle it better than others. Becoming disoriented, blocked from familiar burrows would cause stress, yes."

Duffy shook his head, took off his white kitchen cap, and roughly ruled his mess of hair with active fingers. Duffy smiled at his own surprise.

"All of this behavioral science, called by a fancy name, etiology, evolves, as in the case of the gopher tortoise."

"Evolves?"

"Yes. We humans learn new things all the time, and when they seem to work anew with our caring interaction with the animal world, they should be implemented as new systems."

"Gee whiz, enlighten me. I can't live another minute without knowing."

"There's a comedy show in your future, ole' buddy."

"I know, don't quit your day job," wagged Duffy.

"When gopher tortoises were first moved, the biologists thought they would settle in and burrow new dens fairly soon, the recipient area picked to be so similar to their earlier, familiar habitat."

"And?"

"Instead, they wandered aimlessly, long distances. So, low fences were constructed to box them in somewhat, to limit their wanderings, so they might settle in and construct new digs."

"And?"

"It worked. The authorities leave the low fences up for a few months until their new homes are established."

"Humans using their superior intelligence to help dumb animals."

"Well, I wouldn't put it exactly in those terms, but that is the gist of it."

Duffy glanced at his watch, saying, "We better wrap this up, my regulars will be drifting in soon for early lunch."

"I've got to scoot too. Picking up Lily later today and we're going out to Oak Hill to deliver, hand deliver, Delbert's latest lecture check, at which time I'll tell him about the authorities inviting me and a competent friend to help with some of the relocation."

Dan made quotes with four fingers when he said "authorities."

"A friend of a friend of a friend routine, right! You know everybody."

"Well, I do work often with state and county wildlife folks on a variety of things," defended Dan.

"Of course you do, and I'm proud of you for that," awarded Duffy.

"Thanks."

"Two quick, last questions and then the hot stoves will be calling for me."

"Shoot."

"When do you and Delbert start all this? Tomorrow? Next week?"

"Oh, no, forgot to tell you. That's another important rule. The gopher tortoises can't be captured and moved until we have three straight days of guaranteed constant temperatures of fifty degrees or above."

"Good grief, more stress control?" shrieked Duffy.

"Yes. And, we're still in winter by the calendar, so it will be several weeks yet."

"Oh, brother," said Duffy. "I feel a migraine coming on. Better get that last question out before I have to lie down on the kitchen floor back there."

"What the hell is a sideneck turtle?"

"Oh, they don't live around here. Africa. South America. Australia. They bend their necks sideways when withdrawing their heads back into their shells, instead of straight back."

"Thank God there was no exam today. I would have flunked."

"No, I'm an easy grader," straight-faced Dan.

"You have Delbert's check?" asked Lily. "You wanted me to remind you."

"Picked up at the office from Rosalind over lunch, after I finally got to the office after spending half the morning with Duffy talking gopher tortoises."

"Good."

"Right here in my shirt pocket," patted Dan.

"Fine. I called Mae Ella, saying we would be there by three o'clock. Well over two hours to sit overlooking that pond until dark, devouring Mae Ella's marvelous snacks and some hot chocolate she told me about."

"Super," glowed Dan. "Sure hope those visiting sandhill cranes are around that pond again."

"Your dutiful live-in secretary can report they were there at noon. Naturally, I asked her."

"Maybe we'll get lucky and have them still there."

"Hope so."

"What's the temperature look like this evening, Madam Meteorologist?"

"Should be clear. Fifty-two degrees by nightfall. Perfect stuff. Light jacket and plenty of hot chocolate."

"And, she knows we're bringing Humphrey, to give him an outing."

"She knows and she said she was excited to see that wonderful little boy again."

"Great. Okay. We're set. You have some trail mix and water in your purse as always for us!"

"Of course. When have I ever forgotten?"

"Never," smiled Dan.

"Correct you are."

"You want to drive, or me?"

"You. You've been lounging all day with Duffy. You ought to be well rested except, of course, your lips and mouth, dear."

"How did you know that I did most of the talking with Duffy?" smirked Dan.

"Gee whiz, born yesterday I guess," Lily barbed playfully.

Dan took well her little, harmless sarcasm. They were very much in love and very often it showed its treasured circumstance.

"Besides, I've been on computer all day dressing up my Greek playwright lecture. You know comedies and tragedies."

"Which one wins with the students?"

"Oh, tragedies. More suspense and intrigue, I believe."

"Maybe the ancient Greeks didn't like comedy as much because life was so hard back then without television, cell phones, microwaves, and such!"

"Silly," awarded Lily.

"I'll drive and I'll even stay awake."

"Better you and me in your traveling billboard, the Land Rover. Good for business. Besides, I'm down a dress size and may need some new classroom duds, so I'll act like a pampered queen today and let you honor me by driving."

"I've noticed. Whistle stuff."

"Keep business moving upward," winked Lily.

Humphrey, their marvelous Maltese, now approaching age ten, and senior dog status, was loaded into one of his many mobile carriers, wearing his harness around his torso, his anchor for future leash attachment. Many years before they had stopped the use of a neck leash, learning that the Maltese breed was so susceptible to trachea damage with the normal pull associated with collar and leash.

Dan's *Real Florida Outdoors* Land Rover, one of seven company vehicles, sported its familiar black bear and panther logo, on two magnetic signs displayed across the two front doors, and a painting of a cypress dome hammock neatly displayed across the rear door. All the company Land Rovers were orange-tan and forest-green in color, tributes to Florida wiregrass and forested backcountry. The company vehicles were quite recognizable traveling the highways and byways all across Central Florida.

On the rear floor was Dan's ever-present roadkill equipment. Heavy canvas bag with its airtight zipper, as roadkill was often rancid and putrid. A square-faced shovel and a round-point spade. A long, stout snake hook. Loops of strong cord. A duffel bag filled with dozens of dispensable rubber gloves and sanitized masks, and several canisters of air freshener. Several unopened plastic jugs of water, used to wash down roadkill stains were also on board.

Dan hated unsightly roadkill. He firmly believed, and debated the rightness or wrongness of his theory many times, that cleaning up and disposing of roadkill later for burial kept the driving public less accustomed to ignoring roadkill as simply routine. He knew, of course, that there would remain extensive roadkill along Central Florida roads despite his best efforts to remove slaughtered animals when he saw them along the roads he traveled, but it made him feel good to gather up remains he chanced to see, often sending mobs of vultures flapping away with loud shouts when he began the dirty process of cleaning up where critters had fallen, prey to so many speeding tires. He realized full well that his actions were viewed as downright bizarre by many; but, nevertheless, he felt strongly about his contention that less roadkill grotesquely left to rot or to be pillaged by opportune scavengers made the sad condition ever so slightly a rarer circumstance noticed by the passing public and subconsciously a trifle more acute in the minds of basically good folks who, in large numbers, could make an infinitesimal difference.

He had often said during hot debate with folks, "I fully realize what I do is not earth-shaking at all, but if more people did the same, it might become a factor in producing better results for critters living longer."

Sometimes folks, seeing his obvious deep conviction, weighted this remark and often nodded thoughtfully as they scurried and sought to change the awkward subject.

During the twenty-four mile trip to Mae Ella and Delbert's modest cottage in Oak Hill, he stopped only once, an opossum had been squashed probably that afternoon, perhaps within an hour, as the sky-roaming vultures had not yet discovered the crushed carcass.

Dan unloaded his retrieval equipment quickly, even leaving the motor running in the Land Rover, and with his square-faced shovel soon had the gory remains zipped safely into the sturdy canvas bag. He was back behind the steering wheel, hands washed along with the pavement death scene with most of the water splashed from a gallon jug.

Lily had remained silently in the Land Rover. She wasn't terribly thrilled with Dan's obsession with roadkill removal, but she never spoke up against it, knowing her beloved husband's passion for proaction in this matter was genuine and heartfelt.

Mae Ella and Delbert were sitting close together on the front steps of their bungalow, sharing a pealed orange when they arrived. They had communicated with Delbert by cell phone, his new, strange toy that Dan had given him as a part-time employee favor. Their estimated arrival time was within seconds of prediction. Mae Ella and Delbert had heard them approaching on the lonely, bumpy road and were already waving when they appeared past the last aging Australian pine in a half-mile row of fragile and withered pine brotherhood that had been planted sixty-five years earlier, their heyday for addition to many east-central Florida locations as windbreak measures against howling storms.

Mae Ella's bungalow, as well as two other small homes, had been built at the same time as the planting of the pines, along the lonely, narrow road close to the intercoastal waterway. Mae Ella's parents, Floyd and Florence Tuttle, had been the first owners and Mae Ella had been born there on a weary sofa in 1953 with the assistance of a white-haired country doctor toting a well-creased and faded black bag, who had driven hurriedly up from Titusville when Daddy Floyd had frantically called him from the wall telephone in the only grocery store in Oak Hill.

"Made good time," smiled Delbert, nodding to Lily and extending his ever-friendly, calloused hand to Dan.

"We buzzed right over," said Lily. "Just over twenty-four miles like it always is."

"How many roadkill stops?" chanced Mae Ella.

"Lemme guess," blurted Delbert.

"Go ahead," allowed Dan in a sober tone.

Delbert regarded him carefully for several moments, looking for hints of any kind. With nothing relayed by Dan's deadpan expression, Delbert picked his number.

"Three."

"Nope," said Dan, shaking his head. "One."

"I was gonna say one. No fibbin'. Don't know why I done said three."

"Lemme guess the critter," pursued Delbert, almost reverently.

"Fine," agreed Dan, shrugging without a smile.

"A 'possum."

"Yes. An opossum. Grown but not too old. A hideous sight. I think he showed almost all of his sixty-four teeth, laying stone cold there in the road."

Silence reigned.

Mae Ella broke their funereal solitude with a cheerful suggestion.

"Sandhill cranes are back. Two. They were fishing in the pond out back just a couple of minutes ago. Let's go watch. Quietly."

"Sounds good," awarded Lily, already following Mae Ella around the side of the house with mimicking baby steps. Delbert and Dan followed their measured procession, silent as well.

As they gingerly progressed, not wanting to disturb the sandhill cranes, who were naturally skittish in close proximity to humans, Dan reached into a pocket of his windbreaker jacket and withdrew a plain envelope that held Delbert's paycheck for the previous month, his reward for providing Florida color for three

77

very well-received lectures. He handed the envelope to him.

"You said you was a-bringin' it. Lordy knows, hand deliver by the big boss. I usual get it in da mail."

"You earned every penny. The audiences love you. People, all the time, call ahead of the announced lectures, just to see if you will be on the program."

"Aw, gaw on, ain't so," replied Delbert modestly.

"I'm serious. Just like that. The phone jumping off the hook."

"Can't be a-happenin'."

"I wouldn't lie about something like that. No purpose. You're a natural. Fresh and genuine and all those indispensible good things."

"Well, plenty nice to hear. I trys to do good."

"Just be yourself, like you do. It comes out like old Will Rogers. Just don't get the big head on me. Deal?"

"Can't never do that. Jes plum thankful God has a place for me in his big ole' kingdom."

"He does. You're a big part of his master plan."

Mae Ella had four high-backed, wooden lawn chairs side-by-side up near her rear porch, as far away from the pond as she could arrange them and still be outdoors. They all sat down slowly, maintaining their silence. The chairs were mismatched in color and one was downright rickety. Delbert selected the unsteady chair, of course, without any suggestion from Mae Ella.

The sandhill cranes didn't disappoint. Their natural show was in progress, lean back and enjoy stuff, reels of legend in real time. Really, a live stage show was their treat rather than any spliced-together theater movie. The two sandhill cranes, displaying their smart red forehead caps, male and female, companions for life, were fishing. They slipped through the shallow, tannic water like robotic puppeteers, graceful as ballerinas. Their darting, sharp beaks struck faster than the spellbound human eye could follow. Often, they missed their mark; but, more often, they scored, impaling minnows and surface buzzing insects, surprised selections for dinner.

For fifteen minutes, the two sandhill cranes paraded back and forth in the shallow water that was littered with islands of fading weeds and floating brown debris from an overhanging tree. The cranes were aware of their audience, keeping their distance at the far side of the pond.

Then, in a flash, they were up and away together, heads and graceful necks outstretched and long legs trailing. As they soared skyward they left their patented call behind as firm testimony to their visit.

Kkarooo! Kkaaroo!

They cried their signature call that could be heard for miles in the usually quiet, backcountry Florida.

Delbert broke their collective silence with his own spirited imitation of their famous, hallmark cry.

"Kkaaroo, Kkaaroo," he trumpeted, cupping his work-chipped hands to his mouth.,

"Say, ole man, you copy good," laughed Dan. "You sound just like them. Perfect copy. We need to do a sandhill crane lecture at the auditorium with you sounding off like you were born with feathers."

"I heard 'em all ma life. Know 'em good. Weren't no trouble callin' afer 'em. 'Cept them cries go long past me bein' heared. Miles past."

Yes sir, we've got a sandhill crane lecture in our future, good buddy," affirmed Dan.

"People will love that one," encouraged Lily. "They are elegant birds."

Lily's little audience nodded vigorously, smiling broadly.

"Say, I better get around to telling you one of the main reasons we're here, Delbert," said Dan.

"Oh, they're starting to talk shop with the sandhill cranes gone. Mae Ella, have you got any new craft jewelry we can look at inside so we can escape and we'll let the boys talk!" pled Lily.

"Sure do. And we might just return out here in a few minutes with some Key lime pie and some hot, hot coffee for the four of us while we watch twilight descent over the pond."

"Super," said Dan. "We won't be long. Promise! Especially with Key lime pie coming along."

Mae Ella led Lily inside to her craft jewelry preparation room, but first she showed Lily the new, elaborate quilt she had recently started.

"Delbert, do you remember all the great times we've had in the past, either together trying to help out with things important, or me placing you alone in the direction of something really worthwhile?"

"Sure do!"

"You guarding those ancient dugout canoes from thieves north of here when the long drought exposed them, you and me helping with those tough, tough forest fires over here in Brevard, you tackling that escaped emu with that fish seine, all of us helping with tree and limb deadfall over on the Ocklawaha! Much more!"

"Sure do."

"Well, I've got another adventure for us, coming up soon!"

"Let's heard it. I'm plum excited already," exclaimed Delbert, clapping his hands together as he screamed aloud another sandhill crane cry.

"Listen to this. I've been asked by the powers that be, so to speak, the authorities in charge, whom I have known for years, to assist in an important gopher tortoise relocation program along that Wekiva stretch of new beltway scheduled to be completed. And, they said I could bring along a qualified friend. A couple of them actually mentioned that any qualified person I might bring along could be you."

"No foolin'."

"See how vast your reputation is, ole buddy!"

"Well, count me in. I knowt a good bit now 'bout that there law over protectin' them tortoises. Findin' new homes for 'em. When do we start?"

"Then you are on board, when we get the call?"

"Tomorrow, okay?"

"No. No. Not tomorrow," laughed Dan, "You're too anxious."

"Darn tootin', let's go."

"The law says we have to wait until we are assured of three straight days, seventy-two hours, of temperatures not falling below fifty degrees fahrenheit. Stress relief for the tortoises, not subjecting tortoises to cold in addition to the stress of losing familiar ground, their burrows. This being late January, the thermometer will probably give us the green light some time in late March."

"Can't wait. Can't be soon 'nough. Thanks again, always, for thinkin' of me in dem adventures we keep a-havin'."

"Always," saluted Dan.

Mae Ella and Lily returned outside, Mae Ella carefully balancing a tray holding four large wedges of Key lime pie trimmed with whipped cream and four Styrofoam cups. Lily carried, at arms length, a hot pot of coffee and plastic spoons, forks, and napkins in her other hand.

"I did coffee instead of hot chocolate. Hope, Okay," apologized Mae Ella.

They settled back in silence again, as they had been earlier with the sandhill cranes close by them in the pond. The only sounds coming from the four of them were moans of satisfaction with the delicious Key lime pie and steaming hot coffee, just the ticket for enjoyment outside, on a cool January evening.

Policing his mouth for pie crumbs with a napkin, Dan asked Mae Ella, "You folks got anything brewing for excitement out your way here, anytime soon?"

"As a matter of fact, we do. We're going next weekend to a little local rodeo, one we have been to twice before. You know, we're smack in the middle of horse and cow country here, and out Maytown Road there's a private little ranch where they do most the same things the big rodeos do, but on a much smaller scale. Maybe a hundred folks or so, with their kids, horses, dogs and cows, having a great time. Nothing fancy. No fanfare. Just a happy treat. Looking forward to it. Most people bring a favorite food dish and something to sit on. I'm taking one of my favorite casseroles and we'll cheer everybody on from a little grandstand they have on the ranch. Mostly it's the grown kids who do the competing. No media. Just a bunch of neighbors getting together on the weekend with their friends and families. Secluded and really neat."

"Delbert, you aren't going to be busting any horses or bulldogging any steers, right?" scolded Dan, quite serious with a friendly warning.

"Naw. Too old. Besides, you need me not all broke up, bones and all. Gots to be in one piece, a-helpin' take care of them gopher tortoises wit you."

CHAPTER V

"We'll ice everything down in the big cooler," declared Mae Ella. "I transferred the big store bags into smaller bags and we'll put ice packs around the corners. The two casserole dishes will be fine. They're covered well. No melting leaking into them."

"You a-puttin' dem in da ranch house fridge anyways, oncet we get over to da Nortons?"

"Sure. Inside fridge with the rest of the other food. They have a second fridge if need be."

"Ain't no problem. Ain't but twenty-one miles. Done remember from last good time we had over to dat Norton rodeo."

"Honey, you have the good chairs in the Econoline?"

"Them two best craft show chairs."

"And the big umbrella too, because it will be hot in the sun. It's supposed to be sunny all day, the news said last night."

"Yup. Big umbrella in. Seat cushions too. A whole lot of sittin', fun, but sittin' a bunch of time, if you ain't one of dem cowboys a-showin' off."

"Okay! You promised. You sound a little sorry for yourself, not actually participating in this country rodeo today. I remember you almost took up a challenge last time we went to get into one of those so-called timed events, and you in your sixties with no rodeo experience whatsoever!"

"I rode horses. Plenty of time, whenst I were a kid."

"A kid! How long ago was that?"

"Ole Ike was da president. Ain't too long ago. Wished we a-had him in 'Nam."

"I could have wrung that cowboy's neck, needling you on, making fun with his bragging talk, urging you on. Found out later from Fran Norton that he knew all about your reputation in the Wahaweechee. He was just jealous of all your backcountry success and reputation, growing bigger over the years.

"Ain't nuttin' to it," defended Delbert modestly.

"Well, it's the reason we stayed away the next two years. Now you're three years older and every more reason not to be thinking about racing horses and roping bulls."

"I coulda done dat dare team ropin'. When it were a-runnin', it don't look so tough to me. I coulda run da barrel race too, easy 'nough."

"Fran called the last two years asking us to come. I begged off, afraid you were going to sneak away from me up there, put on a cowboy hat and go match racing and then fall off right in front of me, breaking every bone in that old, but still great-looking body of yours."

"Naw, I behaves myself this time, But, I knowt I ain't too old ta be no cowboy. But, I listens to you good."

"Yes. That's what I want. I don't want you all broke up. Cowboying is for young men."

" I ain't plum old yet," bragged Delbert.

"No, but too old for rodeoing."

"Well . . ."

"You promised Dan too, just days ago when he and Lily were over. You are there to watch only and not be a volunteer cowboy. Besides, Dan needs you fit and strong for that gopher tortoise relocation project coming up soon."

"Done say I be a-sittin' like a good boy, pleasin' my baby, ma Mae Ella."

Delbert went outside, closing the front door just a trifle louder than usual. He and Mae Ella never really fought, they enjoyed the fruits of a superb late life marriage. However, with advancing old age, Delbert wafted grumpy for short spells on rare occasions. These moments were never directed at Mae Ella but rather introspectively toward himself.

Outside, he checked the cloudless, blue morning sky, murmuring to himself, "Gonna be a sunny and real cool day." He checked the Econoline for a third time and found, for the third time, everything in order for their day trip over to the Norton Ranch for the unpublicized, by-invitation-only rodeo.

Only the big ice chest with Mae Ella's delicious casserole creation needed to be added aboard and he would lug it out and lodge it in its place, shored up in the back against the chairs, when they locked the front door ready to leave. Their two cats, brindled Waha and marmalade Weechee, had been fed and their litter box refreshened and placed in its normal kitchen position, where it might or might not be used, cats being more independent and much harder to train than dogs.

Mae Ella cracked the front door and called out that the big ice chest was ready and she was ready with it. Delbert gathered up the heavy polar container and, with a single short grunt, transported it to the rear of the Econoline. Mae Ella exited and locked the front door, wiggling the door knob for added safety. She carefully stepped down the creaking front steps, balancing an armload of jackets and hats.

"Looks like we are feeding the whole county, doesn't it?" joked Mae Ella, in response to Delbert's last ice chest weight gasp.

"Don't it," smiled Delbert.

"Really just us and a few other folks who love my casseroles."

"Yup, us and 'bout a dozen more folk."

"Known for my cooking," she sighed proudly.

"Ain't dat da truth."

"Got the binoculars, babe?"

"Both, in da glove c'parment."

"Good. We're set. Lets go rodeoing. Correction! That is, let's go rodeo watching, as in happy fans looking on."

Delbert nodded weakly.

The trip to the Norton Ranch, a half-hour drive along narrow, asphalt secondary roads, turned up little traffic, until they drew near to their destination. They spotted wild turkey foraging alongside one road and whitetail deer sprinting through a low blanket of winter fog as they whisked along on another forested byway.

Only one roadkill was passed, an armadillo that had attracted a squad of persistent vultures. Delbert didn't stop to collect the roadkill. Normally, he would have done so, taking his lead from Dan, but he reneged on his self-imposed chore this day, with food in the

Econoline and their need to arrive early enough for a convenient parking spot.

Delbert was quiet during their drive, but he responded to Mae Ella's strategies to unleash his normal, talkative nature with polite, if unelaborate conversation. Mae Ella was cagey with her masterful persistence in attempting to derail any lingering thoughts he entertained about actually participating in the rodeo.

"Remember, honey, those pages of sheet music they passed around last time? Fran said over the phone they were doing the same this year. Remember all of us singing "Home on the Range," the "Farmer and the Cowboy," from the musical *Oklahoma*, our National Anthem, the "Battle Hymn of the Republic," "Dixie," and others."

"I 'member."

"Fun, wasn't it?"

"Sure were."

"And, I remember Marty Robbins singing his long, famous song, "El Paso," over that scratchy sound system they had. Static and all ruining that phonograph."

"Yup. I 'member."

With a glimmer of new life in Delbert's mood, Mae Ella plowed ahead with her own quietly stirred cocktail of enthusiasm.

"Do you remember that last page of those long song sheets they had put together? They had typed up and then copied, not song words, but a short history of how rodeos got started. I kept my copy in a stack of that year's letter correspondence and I reread it last week when I knew for sure we were going."

"I see it before, back then. Out West, weren't it?"

"Yes, so interesting. During the long cattle drives out West, in the 1880's, it all got started. When two or more cattle outfits met on the trail going to market, the cowboys started competing to break up the long monotony and hard work of driving cattle. The cowboys started competing in saddle bronc riding, steer roping, and speed events on their horses. Did you know that the American Quarter Horse is the fastest horse for 440 yards, a quarter mile? That's where they got their name. They were bred because the quick bursts of speed were important when herding and controlling cattle."

"I read about it in dat dare music stuff."

"Yes, I thought you did that day. They said in that little bit of history they gave to us that the first rodeo for people looking on was in El Paso, Texas, in 1883."

"Them cowboys jest picked it all plum up, sumphin like kids today playin' pickup basketball in a city park, or kids gettin' up a scrub game of baseball on a sand field. Them call it 'sandlot baseball'. Stuff done grow from early stuff."

"Say, I heard from Dan and others that you were quite some baseball player when you were young. Very good, I've been told."

"Guess I was. Feel like I was. But never got no pro chance. When that dare robber skunk shot momma at da store, I hadta drop outa school and earn a livin' forin all us kids, ma three sisters and me. Then, I wents to war and got bullet nicked in da shoulder. Never had no chance after dat. Done pass me by."

"Yes," said Mae Ella lovingly, placing her left hand on his right shoulder as he drove. She patted him, thrilled to have him talking again, avidly on any subject, even this sad flashback. Anything to bring back his talkative self she would settle for, knowing that once talking, he would gravitate toward sunny enthusiasm, his almost perpetual mood.

When they arrived at the Norton Ranch front gate, which was open and tended by a ranch hand, Delbert left the heavy ice chest there on the ground with Mae Ella to guard while he parked the Econoline outside the perimeter fence of the ranch about a hundred yards down the dusty clay road. He would easily lug the two sturdy folding chairs and their good-sized shade umbrella back to the entrance where the special food chest was being babysat by Mae Ella.

"Howdy, partner," greeted the ranch hand when laden Delbert plodded up through dewy wet grass to join Mae Ella.

"Cliff Travis," he said, extending a calloused paw to both of them.

"We's be Mae Ella and Delbert Turner, pleaseta know ya," returned Delbert.

"You're Delbert Turner, living and breathing, *the* Delbert Turner?"

"'Spect so," mumbled Delbert, shyly hanging his head.

Mae Ella smiled broadly.

"You're a legend in these parts, sir. Honored to meet you. We gotta talk later. Would you take the time, I mean if you ain't too busy with bigwigs out here, to spend a few minutes talking. You sure are a true legend. You make these woods and the rivers speak like they were alive."

"Don't know no bigwigs. Sure we can talk some between them rodeo events we's be treated ta see."

"I'll look you up as the day goes along."

"Fair 'nough."

"Are you folks wanting the grandstand where the judges are or do you want to take your chances on the grounds with your chairs and umbrella there?"

"We prefer the grandstand," responded Mae Ella quickly. The higher the better so we can have a

89

great view all day. We just brought the chairs and umbrella in case you were swamped with folks and we couldn't get up into the grandstand."

"I've got two seats in the grandstand just for you and Mr. Turner. I . . . I . . . mean Mr. Delbert. Uh, I mean Delbert."

"Wonderful," glowed Mae Ella.

"Happy to help," said young Cliff. "And, I got to meet a famous man too," he added with a radiant smile.

Delbert looked away into space, uncomfortable that he couldn't find a nearby hole to hide in.

"Do we need to claim our seats now? We don't want to lose them, but we need to take some food over to Fran in the ranch house for later."

"You do what you need to do. I'll hold your place, and will guard it, but don't take too long, we're set to get started in thirty minutes or less with the flag pledge and singing the National Anthem together."

Delbert stowed the heavy ice chest behind the little, wooden grandstand with all the other coolers, big and small, and at Mae Ella's careful instruction, he lifted the casserole dishes wrapped well in aluminum foil up and out, cradling both wonderfully aromatic creations in both arms as he and Mae Ella made their way to the ranch house, nodding and greeting folks as they walked.

"Hi, ya'll," gushed Fran, all arranged in her best cowgirl attire, sparkling with spangles and rawhide braids, fancy duds she drew proudly from her closet once a year for their country rodeo bash. Eleven years in a row in late January, they had staged their community event, a hoot-and-holler, scaled-down true rodeo that was avidly anticipated for months in the happy expectant minds of about 120 folks in rural Brevard County.

With several neighbors arriving with their own special food delights, Mae Ella and Delbert were shown where to place their casserole dishes in one of the two commercial-sized refrigerators that loomed side-by-side in a utility area inside the garage of their rambling, cypress and yellow-pine ranch house. Other times of the year, the big refrigerators housed veterinary medicines, gallons of water and an array of special diets for some of the 36 cows, 8 horses, and 42 goats that populated their spread. Freshly-cut vegetables from Biff's tendered garden also took up temporary residence there until they graduated to the ranch kitchen.

Biff and Fran Norton called their getaway, in the boondocks, fifty-eight acres west of Oak Hill near the Farmton wilderness, "Palmetto Paradise." That was the official name and that was how mail was addressed to them and delivered. Close friends agreed they couldn't have picked a more fitting name.

Palmetto Paradise was a working ranch, if one stretched the definition a trifle. But a better name would be a "play ranch." The pasture animals, together with the roving, pecking chickens and the squawking ducks all had names, the beloved animal children of Biff and Fran, who had not been blessed with children of their own. Occasionally, one of their big bovine or equine babies died, got terribly sick or took lame and had to be euthanized, but the animals were so much a part of family, they were never sold commercially or even to friends.

Biff took in a few dollars each year, selling honey from the few hives he kept and marketing, jars of homemade horseradish, candled eggs, beefsteak tomatoes, and firewood cut from the one wood lot on the premises, a dense, nine acre tract at the rear of the spread. Mostly, Palmetto Paradise was a play ranch. Both Biff and Fran rode horses around their pride and joy as often as possible and knew every square inch of their property. They counted sandspurs, knowing literally where all the thorny patches seemed to flourish, despite concerted efforts to dispose of them for good.

They employed Cliff Travis and another young fellow, Billy Morrow, both of whom lived with their families in nearby Edgewater. Their main foreman, Bunky Ferris, aged 64, was an old, cracker salt with a noticeable limp from motorcycle days of youth, who did just about everything that needed doing anywhere on the ranch. Bunky was part carpenter, part blacksmith, part cowboy, part veterinarian, part electrician, part mechanic, but his best part was his perpetually sunny and cheerful personality. He had worked at Palmetto Paradise for twenty years after losing his wife to cancer at an early age. He lived at Palmetto Paradise in a small bunkhouse attached to the side of the one stable on the premises. Biff had all the comforts of home installed for Bunky, plumbing, electricity, heat, and even a good-sized television, that Bunky switched on every evening of the year, keeping the volume very low so the horses could sleep in the stable on the other side of his bunkhouse wall.

Biff and Fran, both in their mid-fifties, earned their chief income in Edgewater, up near New Smyrna, 14 miles from Palmetto Paradise, where they had a shop on US-1. Biff was a master plumber, roaming the back of the shop when he was there tinkering, but usually he was out on a leaky faucet assignment with one or two of his helpers whom he hired, part-time mostly and full time some, when he lucked into a commercial building or motel job that required more expertise and attention.

Fran ran the front of the shop, a modest floor-planned appliance center, refrigerators, ranges, dishwashers, washing machines, dryers that they

92

presented as retail from a major hardgoods supplier, who had worked with the Nortons for years, the supplier earning small potatoes for their corporate pocketbook but sweet, sweet potatoes in the form of returned loyalty and totally worry-free business relations.

From inside the ranch house garage, Mae Ella, Delbert, and everyone else there storing food heard a bugle call resound close by outdoors, the yearly signal that the proud community rodeo was ten minutes from officially starting. Biff and Fran overlooked very little at their yearly bash that they truly loved organizing and holding for neighboring Florida cowboys and plain, good ole country folks who loved dressing up and playing cowboy and cowgirl for a day every January, rain or shine, and despite how chilly it was some years.

Folks scurried out from the ranch house, nearly at a trot, hurrying to the makeshift rodeo arena and tiny grandstand that looked so out of place, jutting skyward with sitting room for perhaps only a hundred spectators. The blare of the bugle alerted everyone twice more as people scrambled to their seats or staked their claim to good viewing spots with their folding chairs arranged on the ground near the grandstand.

True to his fawning word, Cliff Travis had placed two reservation placards on the top row of the grandstand, on the side nearest the horse and bull shoots, perhaps the very best seats at the Norton rodeo. He had scrawled Delbert Turner across both pieces of white poster page. In his exuberance over meeting the Wahaweechee Wizard in living flesh, he had completely forgotten Mae Ella's name.

Biff, who had greeted Delbert and Mae Ella at the ranch house minutes before, half-laughing when he said "What's kept you gone two years?", led the salute to the flag. Mae Ella had fielded his inquiry with a firm answer, "I was afraid Delbert was going to try to ride some big, mean bull, that's why, Biff," she said with a brisk shake of her pepper-and-salt hair peeking out below the rim of her cowgirl hat. Biff had smiled silently, leaving the topic without further pursuit.

Folks reverently stood for the flag pledge and remained standing while a ninth-grade young girl with a sweet soprano voice and blonde curls entered the arena astride her well-groomed palomino and, after dismounting, sang the Star-Spangled Banner, with only one small mistake, proving, once again, that our National Anthem is certainly a tough group of words to remember. A Baptist minister from nearby Mims to the south, offered a prayer for the sixth consecutive year, driving up to happily oblige the Nortons, members of his church.

After the ancient sound system, sitting on a shaky table at the bottom of the grandstand, was tested and found to be reasonably satisfactory and screech proficient for another year, Biff called for the procession of horses and riders from the local 4-H Clubs to parade around the dusty, clay arena to signal the real beginning of the festivities. They pranced around carrying the Florida state flag and Old Glory too, trying desperately to stay in line as they had been repeatedly coached. The bugle belted forth some additional strident notes to make sure the living and the dead stayed alert and awake.

The first few rodeo events were comparatively tame ones, nothing too gasping or cliff-edged for the eager crowd, no cowboys flung in the air being bucked off snorting horses or wailing bulls. These were the timed events in cowboy jargon, contestants completing required tasks against the tick of the stopwatch. However, any rodeo event carries danger and the possibility of serious injury with it to the arena.

"First up," fairly shouted Biff, choking the microphone, "is calf-roping."

With calf-roping, a cowboy on his horse chases a calf, trying to rope it with a lariat toss. If he is successful with that tricky chore, the rider dismounts quickly and with his trained horse backing up to keep the rope taut so the calf can't break free, the cowboy tries to throw the calf to the ground and tie three of its legs together.

There were four contestants and the winner with the lowest clocked time was Chappy "Slim" Davis, a lanky ranch hand from down St. Cloud way, who, in winning, stretched his consecutive year win streak to four. The crowd, warming quickly to their usual, excited mood, whistled, cheered and stomped their feet on the grandstand's wooden planks, causing the entire grandstand to tremble slightly. "Slim" tipped his white Stetson to the raucous crowd and kissed to their delight his $50 check that Biff handed to him.

Next up was steer wrestling, also known as bulldogging, the only rodeo event that allows a helper to assist the contestant. The steer is released from a pen between the contestant and his helper. This helper, called a hazer, tries to keep the steer running in a straight line so a cowboy can jump from his horse onto the steer's back, when, if successful with his leap, he tries to grab the steer by its horns and wrestle it to the ground, never an easy feat, and certainly a dangerous time for the cowboy and his hazer accomplice.

None of the contestants scored with their rope toss during the steer roping contest, missing each time, with the steers galloping to a trot at the far end of the makeshift arena, while the sullen cowboys drew up their snaking, dusty ropes in hasty coils of retrieval. The little, disappointed crowd clapped politely, wondering what would be the outcome of the event.

Biff met with two of his stopwatch helpers, and after a brief council of rodeo wars, he announced over the balky public address system that they would run the event again in the hope that they could determine a winner.

Almost begging, Biff shouted, strangling the microphone, "I've got a $50 check burning a hole in my shirt pocket here, waiting to give it to some contestant in this event today."

The crowd roared approval, as the cowboys mounted and twirling their ropes impatiently gathered again behind the steer shoots, eager to try their luck again. The first two cowboys on the seldom-conducted event rerun again missed lassoing their steers. The lusty grandstand contingent sighed a collective gasp, but followed their bewildering surprise with a round of applause, at the urge of Biff at the crackling microphone.

The last cowboy, Hank Kirby from Holopaw, Florida, took gauged time in chasing his steer, circling tight loops of lasso above his head and then he let fly a perfect oval that landed perfectly over the steer's horns. Hank was off his roan mount in a flash, and he double-timed up to his kicking captive and roughly flopped the squalling bovine to the ground. Jumping up, he raised his arms high above his Stetson hat and shook clenched fists in triumph. Hank sauntered over to Biff at the microphone, displaying his best victory strut. And, after he was handed his $50 check, he kissed the spending money voucher and waved it high for the cheering grandstand crowd to see.

Biff did not confine participants in his yearly rodeo to only neighbors. There weren't enough qualified rodeo cowboys in east Brevard County to field a worthwhile event. He invited contestants, like Hank Kirby, each year, not rodeo stars from the big national circuit, of course, but nevertheless, legitimate cowboys who participated in the minor leagues of rodeoing all across Florida.

The next event was a change of pace, a fun time, an interlude like the big rodeos use, as staging time is often needed behind the scenes, readying hustle in the barns and shoots, moving things forward for a new series of events.

It was kiddie time, fifteen young cowboys and cowgirls, aged 5-10, were invited to chase a young calf around the arena, trying to snatch a bright ribbon from its tail, so they would win a prize. The kids, in hats and boots too big for them, chased and chased the elusive calf, stumbling facedown into the soft clay, soiling fancy duds. They stomped on hats, their own and others, that had found their way to the ground all across the arena. Great, safe fun, it always was for the sheer delight of the laughing adults as well as the overly exuberant mob of little ones, dashing around and bumping into each other.

Finally, the tiring calf slowed and allowed itself, wide-eyed and howling, to get wedged in one corner of the arena, where an enterprising 7 year-old girl appropriated the bright orange ribbon for her own prize. Weaving her way through the happy throng, she smilingly, reached Biff, dodging fellow hopefuls like an All-American running back. Biff handed her a gift card in a white envelope. She was going shopping with her mother soon.

Then, the cowboys tied another bright ribbon on a goat, and the kids, now beginning to pursue in teams, chased down the bawling goat boxed in an arena corner and retrieved its ribbon.

By now, all the kids were dusty and grimy, so the last kiddie event, the greased pig chase, couldn't add much detergent need for the clothes of the little cowboys and cowgirls. The pig was as elusive as, well, a greased pig. Finally, they surrounded the squealing porcine dasher, and the big cowboys rushed up to assist and end the chase, to the cheering delight of the adults.

"Where's the clown?" asked Mae Ella, turning to Delbert at her side with a quizzical look painted across her charming face.

"The clown and his barrel are always in the arena for this fun event. Remember, the other years we've been here? The clown clowning around, earning laughs too along with the kids," she added.

"You right. I does remember. Don't know," shrugged Delbert, shaking his head.

"Always in the past! Huh! Maybe they changed things around. Strange." Mae Ella also shrugged. "Oh well, we know the clown is here, just not out there now."

Biff pled to his rodeo flock for applause.

"Having a good time yet?" he shouted.

"Y-E-S," they returned, almost in a synchronized chant.

Two more timed events remained before the renowned and dangerous rough stock events were to be staged. The first, team roping, was sometimes referred to as "heading and healing," with two cowboys working together, one, called the "header" roping the horns of the steers, and the other, called the "healer," capturing the hind legs. The teams roped expertly. The winning team was low on the clock, as all teams had a fair chance to win against the tick of the stopwatch. The crowd loved their exacting proficiency, many standing to cheer and whistle.

The next and last timed event, the cowgirls barrel racing, was also expertly run. Five lady contestants performed flawlessly, rounding three large barrels in a cloverleaf pattern without knocking over any barrels. Fifteen barrels remained standing, with only one tottering to stillness after being brushed slightly by the fifth horse to circle the three. Again, the low stopwatch time determined the winner, a close race, with all five contestants finishing within one second of each other.

Now the rodeo took its only scheduled comfort break. Folks cautiously threaded down and out of the grandstand and formed lines at the Port-O-Lets. Some loped around the arena to the ranch house and used the garage facilities there.

"Twenty minutes, folks. Twenty minutes," barked Biff. "Rough stock coming and then we'll eat. Twenty minutes. We've got bucking horses and mean bulls banging against their stalls, waitin' to entertain you good folks. Bareback bronc, saddle bronc, and, of course, everyones' favorite, bull riding."

The crowd hollered and whistled their approval.

"Bad bull riding," Biff fairly shouted with a projected theatrical tremor in his voice.

Delbert helped Mae Ella to the bottom of the grandstand, steadying her descent along the outside rail.

"Thanks, hon," she smiled, safe on the ground.

"Youse treasure goods, can't have ya fallin' none."

Mae Ella squeezed his hand, and would have planted a long kiss had they not been in a crowd.

"I may stay over at the ranch house some, helping with getting the food ready. They always can use some help. I'll make several looksees back this way, to the arena, during bronc riding, and I should be back for the last event, bull riding; although, that event always makes me so nervous. So dangerous!"

"Fine, honey. I'll stay back and pester Biff some and listen inta some of dem cowboys a-talkin'."

"Super."

Mae Ella, at a brisk walk, headed for the ranch house, and Delbert mossied through a throng of rodeo lovers and wound up alongside Biff, who was earnestly holding court with his help group during the comfort break. Biff was busy, as center of attention in his own little world, but he acknowledged Delbert with a broad smile and a slap on his back, repeating what he had said earlier, glad tidings that Mae Ella and he had attended this year.

As Delbert stood quietly, listening to all the cowboy lingo circling around Biff, he felt a tap on his shoulder. Half-turning, he locked gaze with the craggy, sun-punished cowboy that Mae Ella had disliked years earlier, because of his persistent attempt to prod her Delbert some how, some way, into actual rodeoing.

"Got a minute, Delbert?" he asked impatiently.

"Sure does," Delbert replied with his perpetual vulnerable grin.

"We in a bind, big time. Can you help?"

"Uh, er, what cookin'?" managed Delbert, still smiling.

"We got a clown down. He's out behind the barn barfing his guts out. Come on him sudden like. Musta got a plate of old eggs and bad grits this mornin'. He's sick as a dog, wagging his head like somebody hit him with a crowbar."

"Me and ma wife a-noticin' he weren't in da arena da last two events," replied Delbert.

"He plum sick. Awful. Can you help us out, Delbert? Word has it all through these parts that you can do just about anything."

"Whatcha need?" sampled Delbert, with wide-eyed surprise.

"These last events, broncs and bulls, need all the clowns we can get! Would you pinch hit for us and be a clown for the bronc bustin' and bull riding coming up? All us cowboys got Biff's assignments, workin' shoots and holdin' pen detail, many of us ridin' our own self. You can do it. Outriders will be in the arena, giving support in these next events 'cause they dangerous some. But, we could sure use a substitute clown around the staging pen, helpin' keep control on things."

"Well, I ..., I ..., I."

"Ain't nothin' to it. You wave around a little distraction at them broncs and bulls when they get real frisky-like before they are released. You wouldn't be in no arena, no way. Wouldn't need no barrel. You be behind the scenes a little, so to speak. We lost a clown to illness. We need you.

"I ain't never gone rodeoin'," admitted Delbert.

"You do fine. We needs ya. You don't need to do hardly much."

Delbert looked desperately around for Mae Ella, craning his leathered neck to see through the throng of folks. She was nowhere to be seen. Probably helping out at the ranch house, rapidly ran through his mind.

"Lord God," he mouthed aloud, "I need her now." He almost stuttered, with the enormity of the present situation raining down upon him. He nearly reverted to his old ways of speech, conditions that therapy years earlier, had cured, thanks to the prodding of his great friend, Dan.

"Our sick clown, old Everett, got a spare clown shirt and a clean, floppy hat over to the barn. He your size. We can blacken up your face with wash off stuff and plug a fun clown nose on you. You'll do fine. Nothin' to it. Old Everett plum sick and we need a clown around the pens. You da man, Delbert. You da man."

The crusty old cowboy could have sold blocks of ice to Eskimos!

"Well, I …, I …, I rekon it don't do no harm no way. Dem brass in 'Nam used to say, 'learn soldiering best by soldiering.' So rekon I can learn clownin' in a hurry too, to protect dem cowboys, learnin' as I goes along wit it."

The crusty cowboy already had Delbert plodding along to the barn with a coaxing arm slung around his shoulder. As they walked, Delbert made one last attempt to make eye contact with Mae Ella. No dice. She was in the ranch house on the far side of the arena, far out of sight.

In a flash, Delbert's whole countenance changed, as if he had magically donned a suit of medieval armor. His nerves steeled themselves, electrons in his body summoned to a lifetime of serious and dangerous challenges, sprung into action. He was a different person, his eyes gleaming with the heightened prospect of a new challenge.

In the barn, he slipped on old Everett's spare and clean clown shirt and fitted nicely into his backup floppy hat. He had two black spots as large as silver dollars painted on his cheeks and somebody from backstage barn stuck a split-rubber red bulbous nose on him, asking whether the adhesive fit, was too tight or too loose!

"Just right," answered Delbert, now as confident as Julius Caesar going into battle.

The crusty cowboy, stepping back, looked him over, head to foot, saying he looked as good as Old Everett ever did as a rodeo clown.

Delbert surprised everyone by asserting the positive and taking the initiative, the high ground, as they would say in warfare.

"Let me practice a couple of jumps in dat dare barrel, gettin' used to how it feel and test dem hand holts too, even though I wonts be in no arena."

The crusty old cowboy blinked a couple of times in utter amazement at Delbert's transformation. His buddies, tending to Delbert's clown preparation like bridesmaids before organ music, glanced at each other with looks that melded amazement and respect. Delbert jumped in and out of the barrel twice, asked for a little more black in circles on his face, and stated confidently, almost defiantly, "I'm ready, let's go. I be a rodeo clown."

Now it was the crusty cowboy's turn to nearly stutter. "Uh, uh, Biff's back on the hand mike, getting folks back to their seats, bronc bustin' aint far away."

"Let's get out to dem holdin' pens," urged Delbert, starting to drag the heavy barrel across the hard clay floor of the barn.

"You won't need Everett's barrel. Outriders will be in the arena with this upcoming danger. Not a new clown like you," checked the crusty cowboy.

Delbert got positioned at the holding pens just short minutes before the bronc riding events began, just time enough to orient himself to his now happy task and to make one more unsuccessful sweep of eye to find Mae Ella. Then he recalled that she had said she would be back from the ranch house only in time for the bull riding, the final event.

Delbert practiced jumping down off a holding pen fence and then explored the best way to climb back up.

Biff noticed right off that old Everett wasn't old Everett. His mouth fell open in total surprise. But "thumbs-up" all around from the crusty cowboy and his buddies sitting atop a holding pen fence, calmed him a trifle.

Delbert was a smash hit as a rodeo clown, as if he had sat in that old, familiar rocking chair all his life. Cowboys got thrown in bareback bronc riding several times, and there was Delbert, waving his arms and taunting the kicking horses from the comparative safety of the arena fence. By the time the horses, mostly winning over the dust-smeared cowboys, were retired to snorting fulfillment with their stellar performance in upending humans, Delbert, learning fast at warp speed, was almost ready for the rodeo clown Hall of Fame.

Mae Ella made her way back to the grandstand as the dangerous bull riding event began. She started up to their previous seats, hugging the side rail, but not seeing Delbert on the top row and their old seats now occupied, she took a vacant seat midway up, just above Biff and his microphone. She looked frantically everywhere for Delbert. And then her worst fear slid a cold icicle down her spine, exactly at the moment that Biff chose to avert the crowd to a certain clown substitution.

Biff addressed the crowd between bull riders dispatched from shoots riding terror.

"Old Everett, a huge clown favorite for years here took sick about an hour ago. He'll be fine in a little while. Filling in for him now and doing simply great around the holding pens and staging shoots is our own Delbert Turner, famous Man of the Woods, living down Oak Hill way."

Applause couldn't muffle Mae Ella's shriek.

"D-E-L-B-E-R-T!"

Mae Ella stood, blocking views, and shook her fist at Delbert, who was having so much fun squatted atop the fence, he was sweating with active enthusiasm, with black circles leaking down his face.

Mae Ella, defiant and protectively angry, continued to stand during the bull riding events, several minutes, until a patient crowd of onlookers, giving her space as the obvious, concerned wife, finally pled, "Down in front."

Delbert broke into his legendary, disarming grin, the one that captured everyone, and said softly across the table.

"I went rodeoin' didn't I. Gosh darn it, wish I coulda been in da arena, a-hidin' some in one of dem barrels!"

CHAPTER VI

"This storm, a real big one, may not be as bad as what they called 'The Storm of the Century' back twenty-five years or so, but these late winter northeasters that come down through Florida every once in a while look just about like summer hurricanes, they can be so fierce," warned George Mason, owner of Otter Creek Marina, located just outside the south border of the Wahaweechee State Forest.

"I remember that one well," sympathized Dan Miller over the telephone, to his old friend.

"So, with a little notice on its dreaded arrival, 36 hours or so, thank God for advances in weather reporting by the way, I called Delbert this morning. I'm going to button up the marina, tighter than a drum, and put all the kayaks and canoes away in the two sheds, up on the racks I seldom use, and ride out this northeaster like it's going to be a hurricane."

"Smart move," agreed Dan. "I guess it will cost you some real money, with the recent mild weather and good, steady kayak and canoe rentals at the marina, I'm sure you have enjoyed in the pocket book."

"Yes. No cash register music. But precaution now in storing away my rentals could be a big pocket book plus, if we have limbs down out here smashing them up where they usually lie on our grassy bank."

"Right on," agreed Dan. "You have a lot of oak understory stretching over your display of rentals. And, some very old oaks among them."

"Weary old oaks. Beautiful but still weary. Big limb breakage with high wind, a real possibility."

"So, Delbert's coming by to help with the button-up?"

"Just hung up with him. He'll be here in three hours."

"Hm'm noon."

"Yup."

"George, is he coming by johnboat or canoe, like in the old days when he had his little lean-to hut at Possum Slough and he paddled down once a week to get his laundry done at your marina while he scrubbed up all your rentals that had been rented out?"

"Funny. Funny. Your sense of humor with the big storm coming," growled George playfully.

"Those who can still laugh in the face of a great adversity have the whole world by the tail," sermonized Dan.

"True. True. I always like your unsolicited pearls of wisdom. You make me feel like I'm going to college now to make up for not being able to go after high school many, many years ago."

"Thanks for the compliment, even though some of it might have been a slight exaggeration."

"No. I mean it."

"Well, thanks then."

108

"No. Delbert's coming by car. Driving around by himself. Mae Ella's at a quilters' work social."

"She stays busy with stuff she loves."

"She loves him and that's a fact."

"No kidding. The sun rises and sets on Delbert in her eyes."

"That's a good thing. Say, how old is he now. I could guess pretty close, I think."

"Just turned seventy-one in February. The 22nd in fact. George Washington's birthday."

"That's fitting. He's the George Washington of our forests and waterways. He bleeds green and blue."

"He does indeed."

"Wow, he's in super condition. Seventy-one. Wow!

"I'd hate to have to arm wrestle him and I'm years younger," allowed Dan.

"For sure."

"Say, you mind if I swing by too? I can lend a hand with the kayaks and canoes. It will go faster with three of us. With the news of the big storm, I've got a little tie-down myself out here at home, but nothing I can't accomplish later today with Fred, our expert caretaker. By the way, did I ever tell you about Fred? Best day's work I ever did, hiring that whiz."

"Several times you have told me all about him. Yes."

"Oh!"

"Sure, come on by. It will work well. Six hands instead of four. When we finish, we'll steal some sandwiches out of the grocery cooler and some drinks. I'll ask Clara to see if she can rustle up some pie and ice cream too."

"Not too much chow, ole buddy, I'll be wanting to grab a nap snoozing on your deck."

Delbert and Dan arrived at Otter Creek Marina, from slightly different directions, within three minutes of each other. They had talked twice by phone, once when Dan passed along his conversation with George and, again, when they were both on the road headed toward Otter Creek.

Dan, arriving first, parked near the marina grocery store that had stocked Delbert with groceries for so many years when he weekly cleaned kayaks and canoes left dirty and messy from weekend usage. Coincidentally, it was a Monday, the usual day of the week in years past when Delbert paddled from his hidden retreat at Possum Slough to perform his two-thirds of a day of work in exchange for groceries for the week. Dan went inside and greeted Clara, George's wife, who had been on many trips and excursions with her husband, Lily, Delbert, Mae Ella and himself. Clara wasn't busy on a slow late winter Monday. Soon, they were laughing and joking about good memories they had shared.

In his purring, nine year-old blue Ford, Delbert soon arrived and parked next to Dan. His family member Ford had a few dents and dings spread around its epidermis, but Delbert, handy with tools as well as all things found in Mother Nature's pantry, kept his aging Ford young and energetic by tinkering over it constantly with love, care, and mechanical savvy.

Dan and Clara met Delbert on the front steps of the marina grocery, and the three of them, jovial in spirit, walked the short distance to George's rental office. George, looking for them periodically through the window walked out of his office to greet them as they approached.

"My helpers have arrived, in your face bad ole storm," he declared, throwing his arms open wide.

"I'm always your helper, thought you noticed," chimed Clara, laughing aloud.

110

"And so you are, my dear," affirmed George with a smirk and a bow. "I guess I mean my special workers today, the heavy lifters," he added.

"Them kayaks and canoes a-liken' family. Jes like kids to me," said Delbert. "Don't want dem hurt none wit dis here storm a-comin'. Let's put 'em up in dem dry sheds."

"I'm here to help," echoed Dan. "Needs doing, being on the side of safe is always good."

"If those kayaks and canoes sustain any real damage out in the open unprotected, we're virtually out of business for a time. They are the attraction here at Otter Creek. We're just flunkies, George and me," pled Clara.

"Truer words never spoken," seconded George. "Regardless of the power of this storm arriving tomorrow, hurricane strength or not, we'll do a hurricane type of fire drill and be on the safe side, like Dan says," rallied George.

"Well, I'm our waiter and chief cook type for lunch when you guys finish," asserted Clara. "Out under the oaks at one of the picnic benches, okay? No bad weather yet."

"Perfect," said Dan. "But, Clara, you are going to be with us, one of us at lunch, right? No waiter needed."

"Of course I will. Try to stop me," laughed Clara. "I'm one of you. I just meant someone has to be in charge of lunch, and that's me. I'm too old to lug kayaks and canoes around."

"We's do that," firmly stated Delbert.

"How long will you be, George," so I can gauge lunch?

"Well, let's see. Forty-one tiny ocean liners to move. Six hands. Walking forty yards to the shed each time. Hm'm. Wish I had liked math back in school. Hm'm. Hour and a half, I'd say, If I were a betting man, Clara. Maybe a little more."

"I'll be ready by one-thirty. Synchronize watches like they used to do in the old war movies," joked Clara.

Dan and George chuckled mightily.

"We's need one of dem stupidvisers," said Delbert, with stony candor.

His expression evoked an explanation request from Dan.

"How do you mean?"

"Even da heavy canoes, da old wooden ones, move best with four hands, one of usins, front and back. Them two extre hands wit three usins don't do no good, no way. Third person in da way and clumsy like for dat third person to carry on by his loneself. We need one of dem lunkhead stupidvisors."

"Well, I'll be, Delbert's exactly right," said Dan with wide amazement, astonished once again at Delbert's uncanny ability to size up virtually any situation.

George didn't want to lose any of his able-bodied help. No way on that. Hastily, he invented a solution.

"Well, we'll trade off and on, two of us on canoes and kayaks, one resting. Good bit of walking with a load, you know. One of us can rest, kind of on break," groped George.

"No problem," shrugged Dan.

"I'll start sweeping out the sheds. They need it. I'll see that the ladders are up, the lighter kayaks go on the top racks. We'll make it work. We'll figure out a system."

"Me better at a-workin'. Ain't much good at being no stupidvisor," said Delbert, as solemn as a minister at a rainy graveside service.

Dan caught George's gaze for only a split second. Both of them deadpanned humor wrapped in respect.

George had two storage sheds at Otter Creek Marina. Both were durable and sturdy with no roof leaks to be found. One, the older, was crafted from cypress and yellow pine, still servicing well beyond its years, and the other was erected with gray sheet metal. Each had a wide double-door entrance and sat raised, above the ground, atop an open foundation. The kayak and canoe racks inside were in good condition, well-braced and secure.

Both sheds were unlocked by George and he readied the ladders in each for the hopefully safe and short storm mothballing transport of his little rental navy. Cordpulling illuminated both sheds with meager but adequate light from bare, overhead bulbs. He decided to sweep each floor space at the conclusion of the moving expedition after the three of them unavoidably had traipsed in all the brown, dead leaves in the county.

Clara had already walked back to the marina grocery to think about lunch preparation before the three moving musketeers decided to stop yapping and really get down to work.

Dan and Delbert started first with their four-hand tandem shuttle of the kayaks, after threading the now unlocked long chain down through the low eyelet of each, so they could be transported individually. In the early going with George pulling the cushy duty as first stupidvisor, the trek to storage shed was swift and lively; but, as the afternoon wore on, Delbert and Dan, both extremely fit for their age, slowed their pace noticeably. It was a mighty chore, and as they progressed, they laughed and joked less and less.

When the twenty-three kayaks were in place, up on the highest racks with George patting each one

113

to rest like a doting, loving mother putting a child down for a nap, Delbert and Dan, sweating like longshoremen on a waterfront dock, took a self-determined ten-minute sit down break.

"Whew," managed Dan, carding torrents of perspiration from his brow, "I'm getting too old for this kind of stuff." Early on, he had removed his trademark hat, leaving the soaked standard on a bench.

"Me too," agreed Delbert. "I'm a-feelin' it too. Shucks, I usta sling dem rentals 'round like matchsticks when I were young an' workin' a day a week for Clara and George. No more! Ole man Father Time done come by to say howdy."

"Truer words never spoken," muttered Dan.

"Right as rain. Gospel true."

"How many canoes we got left with the kayaks done?"

"I done count. Twice! I'm a-lookin' for the end likein youin Dan."

"Less than what we've done. Please tell me that."

"Yup," obliged Delbert. "Only eighteen canoes."

"Over halfway," sighed Dan hollowly.

"And dem canoes a mite more heavy."

"Thanks for reminding me. You could have gone all day without bringing that up, ole buddy."

Dan and Delbert rested in silence for a couple of minutes more, and then looked at each other with that sober stare that meant hard work break-time inevitably ends.

"Let's get moving or I'll freeze up right here like a stone statue," gloomed Dan.

"Yup. Back to it," Delbert sold to himself.

During their slumping break, George had sneaked a little looksee out to their sitting repose, shielding himself by a cracked-open shed door. He had no further chores to putter with in either shed during their upcoming canoe toting ordeal so he decided to store his stupidvisor badge and dive head-first into the caravan movement of canoes.

When Dan and Delbert started lugging the canoes, George was there with them, helping Dan with his end of the first canoe.

Six hands! No stupidvisor!

"Let me pitch in," he demanded earnestly. The last thing he wanted was the loss of his tiring workers, so close to the finish line.

Neither Dan nor Delbert talked George out of helping, during the plod, almost stumble, to the finish, that unforgiving forty yards seemed like a mile each way. George made the transport easier, at either Dan's end of a canoe or assistance for Delbert, at the other end. Conversation had long since devolved from work harmony and frivolity to a mixture of grunts and groans.

The work moved along steadily, six hands were definitely better than four. And, before they actually realized it, they were lugging the last canoe to storm storage just as Clara approached within their peripheral view, laden down with a wicker basket and a Styrofoam cooler.

The three moving musketeers sagged to sighing relief at the picnic bench chosen by Clara.

"I'll sweep out those leaves we dragged in later," moaned George, flapping a weak hand at both sheds.

"Works for me," agreed Dan, as he placed his dry trademark Australian bush hat atop his matted mop of wet hair.

"Them old brown leaves ain't gonna get in no trouble, 'til you get 'round to them," ratified Delbert.

"Well, you boys look like you all have been hiking through Florida swamps. Soaked to the bone. Did somebody spray you all with a hose?"

"Call it the canoe and kayak war. It ought to be given a name as it will stick around in my memory for some time," offered Dan.

"Dem canoes seem a mite heavier now since when I was a-slingin' 'em 'round years ago," chuckled Delbert.

"A great effort. A great effort. You guys fought a storm before the real storm. Believe me, you did."

"Well, what will it be? Grocery store sandwiches, made off-site, fresh from a cooler, all wrapped in cellophane? Or? Or? One of mine hand-crafted in the last hour while you fellas were slaving away with that awesome transport caper? I snuck away to our apartment and made some sandwiches fresh as morning dew, for all of you."

"Make mine one of yourn, Miss Clara," urged Delbert. "Two even ifin you gots plenty."

"Two it is, Delbert. I have eight new sandwiches and four more from the standup cooler."

"Two of yours for me too," seconded Dan.

George nodded agreement.

"Your sandwiches, honey," chorused George. "I know on what side my bread is buttered," he added playfully.

"Better pick mine," answered Clara with a wink.

Clara passed the sandwiches around, two apiece.

"Chicken salad, egg salad, tuna, and ham and Swiss. They're all marked with a first letter. C.E.T. H. See! On the bounty wrap."

The food treasure was distributed like pirates dividing up stolen booty. All fair and square.

116

Everyone got their choices, first and second. No conflict!

The Styrofoam chest was dismantled first. Clara had an assortment of canned soft drinks swimming in ice. They disappeared like new treats found on some deserted island inhabited by three shipwrecked survivors. Conversation became audible moans and groans of satisfaction, until the sharp edge of thirst and hunger was assuaged.

Dan was the first to speak, while still munching the last delectable remnants of Clara's ham and Swiss creation.

"George," he declared in orator fashion.

"Yes, I'm here."

"When this miserable storm passes and it's time to move all your huge navy of canoes and kayaks out again into the noonday sun, I will be in Mongolia. Unreachable in Mongolia. And, I might add, if they have even one solitary telephone there in Mongolia, I'll find someplace even more remote to be."

"That bad, huh?" smirked George.

"That bad! Are there any chiropractic clinics on the New York Stock Exchange? If there are, it's time to buy some stock in them."

"You're not hurt," asked George in a serious tone.

"No, nothing like that. Just kidding. I'm fine. Just feeling sorry for myself, feeling a little old for some honest work that wouldn't have phased me even ten years ago."

"Well, you don't have to hide out in Mongolia. The canoes and kayaks will fly out of the storage sheds with that gang of college boys I hire part-time, doing the job Delbert used to do here years ago."

"Great. The Mongolia trip is officially cancelled."

"How do you feel, Delbert?" asked Clara. "You okay?"

"Me a little likein' Dan. Gettin' old and totin' work like we's just done sure raps an ol-timer on da noggin' wit some hard sense 'bout time a-movin' on."

"But, you're okay, now?"

"Finer den frog hair. Yourn fancy vittles done bring me back. I could tackle more totin' ifin it was a-there ta do."

"So-o-o-o," drew out George. "Next bad storm, after this one, no volunteering from this crew, right?"

"I would say you are exactly on target, ole buddy. How about you, Delbert?"

"Well, ma Miss Mae Ella always got stuff for me ta do at da house an' I still visit to ma nature center some too, a-lookin' for a chore to two needin' doin'."

After a polite pause, George said, "Should I take that as 'No'."

Stone-faced, Dan and Delbert blinked at each other, and then started laughing, George and Clara joined them in a riot of roaring fun.

The three men kicked back at the picnic table, drinking in the gentle buzz of nature. They yawned and propped themselves awake with elbows bracing their chins. Squawking birds appeared, circling overhead, eager to swoop down for scraps if the pesky humans would ever decide to move. The marina was quiet, almost totally deserted. Clara began to police crumbs and confiscate soiled napkins. Hungry men had left her with an empty lunch basket and Styrofoam cooler, once she spilled the meager ice across the grassy lawn.

"Everybody's home or at the super market getting ready for this northeaster," offered George. "That's why we are so alone out here. Happens every time a hurricane threatens too. Like we don't exist. Just hope it won't be too bad."

"Maybe we'll get lucky," grimaced Dan.

"Prayers help," soothed Clara.

Delbert closed his eyes and kept them tightly shut until he realized that Clara wasn't going to say a prayer. George and Dan exchanged slight smiles, courtesy of their deep fondness for Delbert.

After a brief period of quiet, collective reflection, Dan changed the subject with heightened enthusiasm.

"Which brings me . . . which brings me . . . to a main reason I joined this slavery event today, in addition, of course, to wanting to help." Everyone perked up. Dan had a way about him.

"George, I mentioned to you on the phone this morning that I hadn't seen this ole rascal Delbert in more than a couple of weeks, and I was anxious to see him because I had some big news for us. Big, good news."

"Let her fly," enthused Delbert, pounding the picnic table with his fist.

"A new adventure, should he choose to accept. A great, neat new adventure."

"Whoopdedo," shouted Delbert. "Bring her on. What we's gonna be a-doin'."

"Well, should you agree, you and I are going to join some others and do some python hunting in the Everglades."

"Wow, that is big news," said George. "I've been reading all about it. The invasion of exotic species in the Everglades. Non-native creatures, like pythons, causing big problems."

"You betcha," applauded Delbert, his excitement level raising.

"When we a'goin'?" he stammered.

119

"Within thirty days. I'll get the call in plenty of time."

"A friend of a friend of a friend," joked George.

"Well, I'll be," added Clara.

"I guess I'm lucky enough to know some folks in high places in Florida wildlife control. The big honchos. I don't butter them up, I just have a lot of interaction with them in my work at *Real Florida Outdoors*. Things open up naturally. But, almost all things that open up involve plain hard work, never freebee luxuries. Nothing like that. I do admit that some of the things that come my way turn into high adventure, true. But, all in all, you have to stay on your toes and put forth some effort, ingenuity, and inevitable lost time from work."

"Of course," granted George. "I didn't mean anything negative when I said a friend of a friend of a friend."

"I know you didn't," dismissed Dan.

"You know the governor personally, don't you, Dan?" said Clara.

"I do. First name basis, but, here again, our friendship involves volunteerism and philanthropy mostly, not parties or social climbing."

"Never doubted it," approved George.

"Anyhow, Delbert and I are invited to take part in the next python hunt. Airboats! Backcountry! Younger guys will be doing the real grunt work, the up close and dangerous stuff. We'll be behind the scenes some, like we have been in the past, fighting large forest fires near main interstates. Delbert and I have seen one hundred foot flames lick up a big pine and blacken it badly in just a couple of minutes."

"We's sure 'nough have, gettin' a red, hurt face a hundred yards away," documented Delbert.

120

"Oh, we'll see some action in the Everglades. But, old geezers like us will do things like keep statistics, tabulate findings, judge patterns, be observers, close stuff and important, but I doubt that we'll be in any danger of being a python supper."

"I'm in," assured Delbert. "I get my liberty card punched by Mae Ella, and I can add python hunting to my bucket list. Done crossed off rodeoing on dat bucket list. Bring on da python hunting. I cross off dat dare 'venture wit a big smile likein I did a-rodeoin'."

"I heard about that clown caper. You were something. Mae Ella told Lily that she was furious with you."

"Shucks, no, we went to smoochin' and such dat day when we's gots home."

"Oh, okay," laughed Dan.

The group of four unwound themselves from the comfort of the picnic table, stretched and then said their goodbyes.

"Seriously guys, you both were super, coming to my rescue like that with practically no notice," thanked George.

"Remember I'm in Mongolia when those boats have to leave those sheds," joked Dan.

"Got you," assured George, "I'll be making no international phone calls."

Both Delbert and Dan hugged Clara, kissing her on the cheek, as they thanked her for the special picnic lunch.

Dan was off to his Land Rover, checking Lily on his cell phone, asking her to tell Fred he was on his way, in case chores at *Le Terrier de Renard* needed attention before the nasty northeaster arrived the following day.

Delbert hastened also to his Ford pal, calling Mae Ella on the cell phone Dan had given him. He also assured her that he would be right home to secure their humble cottage in Oak Hill against the wind and rain bully that was set to pay a visit.

But, Mae Ella had trouble understanding him. Delbert kept talking excitedly about bucket lists, python hunting and ranting on about could they do some smooching and such, when he got home likein when they had done after he went a-rodeoin'.

CHAPTER VII

"Old man, you have never chased snakes in Florida or anywhere else as big as pythons. Never! And, I've known you since you were twenty-three," stated Lily firmly, sitting on her back porch at *Le Terrier de Renard,* enjoying the parade of pond-centered wildlife, with her lovely arms folded indignantly.

"What's this old man business?"

"I'm rather young and spry for my age, I think."

"Granted. But my old man is way too old to go wading around in the mushy and wet Everglades looking for constrictor beasts like pythons."

"Aw, we'll be fine."

"Oh, sure, you and Delbert. You well know that man will try anything, literally anything. I love him dearly, but he's a bad influence. Recently, you realize, he was in a rodeo for the first time at age seventy-one. Good grief, he'll jump in head first down in the Everglades, all charged up about some slithering giant, and you'll follow or try to follow."

The bull riding went well, without any bad incident for Delbert. He distracted the bulls by yelling and by putting his thumbs in his ears just to mock the huge brutes. Mae Ella, calming a little, only a little, apologized to folks behind her when she was compelled again and again to stand to watch over the safety of her man.

Planks of wood had been stretched over stacks of concrete blocks and the lunch laid out before folks after the rodeo ended would have dwarfed the old banquet feasts of Henry VIII in jolly old England. The dishes of food, the best recipes from all the women attending, were superb as usual.

Mae Ella was holding a seat for Delbert, across from her, with her cowgirl hat as reservation. Delbert slunk over from the barn, after changing back into his own shirt and rubbing off what face paint would come off without employ of a mirror. When he sat sheepishly, like a juvenile's first time in traffic court, Delbert waited for a fusillade of scolding from Mae Ella. However, because he looked so comical, all smeared up with running face paint and wet, matted hair, Mae Ella simply laughed out loud, breaking the cliff-edged worry of a dose of rough, rough scolding.

"Lookee here, babe, old Everett done give me that red nose I was a-wearin'. A keepsake he call it.

Delbert produced the damp with sweat rubber nose from his shirt pocket.

"Ken we's keep it 'round da house someplace?"

Mae Ella studied him for a moment and then, leaning forward, she whispered "Stinker!" But then, moments later, her stern countenance crumpled into a smile.

"I'm proud of you," she bestowed, again whispering.

105

"We won't get into any trouble," assured Dan, in his best soothing voice. "And, honey, he wasn't actually in a rodeo as a contestant. He was a clown, helping cowboys."

"He was all dressed up with face paint and a rubber nose, helping out in the pens and sitting on the fence close to the action, with other clowns. If that isn't rodeoing, what is?"

"Oh, well, they had an emergency and he came to their rescue."

"Those are the words I've been searching for, thanks for the reminder. 'Emergency,' as in emergency room and 'rescue,' as in rescue van.

"Oh, c'mon, honey. You're being too dramatic."

"Tell you what, let's make a deal."

"What's that?"

"You stay home and I'll squeeze and cling to you so much and so often you won't be thinking pythons one bit."

"Say, now that sounds awfully good."

"Try saying 'tempting'."

"Babe, you know I'm committed to my friends in south Florida. Can't back out if I wanted to. We'll be statistic chartists and 'go-fors.' Assistants! I doubt we'll see any close action and the recent hunts have had only fair results down there, not a lot of sightings and confrontations."

"Stay home and enjoy some close action!" smiled Lily.

"Now, babe, you know I would love to do that. Always. We'll only be gone five days or so."

"I ought to tie a knot in my nightgown so tight it couldn't be opened with a chain saw."

"Oh, honey, that's not you," pouted Dan.

"You are responsible for one of the biggest ecotourism businesses in the state. You are the swizzle stick that stirs the drink, making things happen. A lot of people depend on you."

"I know that and I appreciate that responsibility."

"Better."

"I'll be ultra-careful."

"Better again," demanded Lily, still fuming and fussing.

"Say, look, sandhill cranes, other side of the pond. Four."

"I see them," thawed Lily.

"Aren't they marvelous?" stirred Dan in his 'change of topic' ploy. "I never get tired of seeing them."

"Magnificent," softened Lily. "I never tire of watching their antics either."

"Me too," agreed Dan, now with some success in calming his lovely, well-intentioned wife.

It looked as though Dan had successfully switched their topic of discussion away from python hunting with the fortuitous arrival of sandhill cranes at their pond. He edged on cautiously, hopeful to control the atmosphere, as he sat with his wife, holding his breath, happy with her more agreeable mood.

"Say, while we're away for that short time, being super aware of safety, at a distance always, why don't you and Mae Ella officially start putting together some real lasting details on Delbert's big roast coming up?"

"You know, you and I are psychic! No question. I was thinking of just exactly that this morning. Really was."

"Great," exclaimed Dan, not wanting to hear any more python venom from the sharp mouth of his caring wife.

"H'mm. Good idea."

"You have a working date already! October, October'"

"October 20th, a Saturday, eleven o'clock in the morning for salutes and recognition and then what I hope will be a fabulous lunch and personal toasts by many folks after lunch."

"And the Gators on TV?"

"Checked ahead. They play that evening. No conflict."

"Smart, smart lady. As great as Delbert is, and as popular as he is everywhere, you don't want to go up against our Gators, playing in Gainesville or somewhere else on national television."

"I took that precaution," said Lily proudly. "After all, anyone who was invited to the White House Rose Garden for a special award along with a dozen or so other environmental heroes from around the country, needs to be treated like a superstar."

"There were nineteen. All unsung, unassuming superheroes from our troubled planet."

"Nineteen! Of course you would know, babe, you went with him."

"My honor. Wanted to make sure all those big city sounds, trucks, sirens, commotion, didn't bring back Vietnam memories to him."

"I know you were able to settle him. It was daunting enough shaking hands with the President, as shy as Delbert is."

"For certain. I held my breath through it all, but he did fine."

"We gals are going to shift into high gear while you are gone."

"You have reserved the site, the Delbert Turner Nature Center. That's absolutely crucial."

"That much is done, with plenty of caution down there, announcements not, repeat not, to appear in print anywhere down there in the form of a poster or

126

a billboard or a sign. Nothing! This is a total surprise and we'll try our darnest to keep it a total surprise."

"How about the Internet," scoffed Dan muffling a laugh.

"Yeah, Delbert on the Internet. As likely as an asteroid hitting us sitting right here in the next two minutes."

"I'd laugh, but I respect him too much to do that. The fact that Delbert is no tech whiz is of no consequence at all."

"Of course. Of course!" nodded Lily.

"You don't mine me throwing things out, do you? Two heads better than one, don't you think? But... but, it's your show. You, Mae Ella, Clara and the other women totally involved."

"No, I don't mind. And, I love your partially staged enthusiasm to deflect conversation away from pythons in the Everglades. Quite compelling. Nicely done!"

Dan grinned sheepishly. She knew him well. Debate over. He was caught again.

"So, all the incidentals will come later this summer?" Dan summarized quietly.

"Sure. We'll check them off as we go. Early on too. This won't be any last minute scramble. We won't back ourselves into that corner."

"Food. Decorations. Media. Invitations."

"Oh, yes, invitations. That's the biggee. The rest falls into place. Food. Decorations. Even the sound system. No worries."

"You shooting for the moon?"

"From the governor down. Is that moon enough in the universe of invitations?"

"I should say!"

"Time to get rolling, big time. Only six months away."

"In your capable hands, it all will get done, perfectly," sugared Dan.

"Aren't you sweet!" chided Lily. "You just want me to stop ragging on you about going python hunting."

"Python hunting observing."

"Oh, sure, like I was born yesterday," teased Lily.

Dan slipped off the hook again, by changing the subject.

"As you work through this retirement toast process, and that is what it is, a retirement toast, not a roast, I'll help all I can. Postage at the office. Calls made to follow up on the invitations. Things moved to the nature center. Anything."

"No kayaks or canoes moved. Mr. Python Frank Buck."

"No."

"You're too tired this afternoon after your Otter Creek Mayflower Van Lines caper and helping Fred here before this storm, to be frisky. Admit it."

"Babe, I'd rally somehow. I would!"

"Down boy, enjoy the wildlife. Four-legged critter wildlife."

"Aw, shucks, I was just going to sink into a two-minute nap to get back into suitable preparation."

"War of words, you mean!"

Their laughter awakened their six-pound watchdog, their cherished little Maltese, Humphrey, who had been snoozing on his favorite oval rug on the back porch. The sandhill cranes, seeing movement through the screening at the porch, and showing their curiosity for and lack of fear of humans had high-stepped around the small pond to a position near the porch. Humphrey started to bark at them. The double doors were screened totally and when the graceful, avian ballerinas came close, Humphrey growled his annoyance, looking back over his shoulder continuously to make sure Dan and Lily knew all about the presence of those slender, gray invaders with their distinctive red crests, arriving a mite close for the tolerance of one tiny, but strict guard at *Le Terrier de Renard*.

Dan clapped his hands and playfully scolded Humphrey.

"Hush, now. Hush. They mean no harm, Humphrey. You're still the boss of our whole place. But sandhill cranes are beautiful and they sometimes come up to people, so your mom here and I love to see them come up close when they decide to do so."

"His 'mom'! I love it when you say that."

"I'm glad."

"I take as good a care of that little sweetheart as humanly possible, I feel that with all of my heart."

"No question. No question. You are absolutely correct. Devoted to Humphrey."

Lily placed her hand on his forearm and looked deep into his eyes.

"Be careful, really careful on this python hunt. No heroes, okay. Really."

"I promise," said Dan solemnly.

"I believe you. I won't say any more about it. That's my promise to you."

Dan and Lily clasped hands and squeezed hard.

The northeaster was kind and considerate, throwing east-central Florida a generous life preserver that fitted perfectly. Wind wailed and rain pelted most assuredly for several hours, but the intensity was down from the benchmark ferocity of recent late spring storms recorded in bad weather annals going back one hundred years.

Some trees, the sick and nearly dead ones, toppled in many areas, and blankets of twigs and

Spanish moss spread across neighborhood roads and yards of homes, interspersed with fallen limbs of all sizes, but the commercial damage to buildings and store fronts was limited greatly, a circumstance that pleased mostly everyone except the cleanup crews which appeared out of thin air to prey upon the weather disadvantaged, negotiating their usual exorbitant prices, while smiling diabolically.

As became the fortunate norm with the storm across central Florida, George and Clara Mason sustained only modest inconvenience at Otter Creek Marina. The hearty college help moved the canoes and kayaks back out from the sheds to the rental line without the huff and puff endured by Dan and Delbert. They picked up armloads of Spanish moss loosened from trees and small limbs that had snapped and fallen to the ground after they had the undamaged ships for hire back at their enticing best for the river-venturing public.

Le Terrier de Renard was festooned too with clumps of wind-dislodged Spanish moss and a carpet of twigs and small limbs spread across the manicured patches of grass beginning to green for their boast of spring. But Fred, with Dan's help, had the charming seven-acre homestead sparkling again with no more than a dozen full wheelbarrow trips to the front property line where county trucks would collect and dispose with their normal pickup service.

Dan and Delbert saw a great deal of each other in the days following the storm that had demonstrated restraint and favor. They participated in a gopher tortoise relocation, their second invitation to be a part of one of those decisive change of scenery missions that meant continued life for the shelled critters, and, in that sane process, humans won their goal with their dubious passion for development.

Delbert was at his usual animated best, exploring gopher tortoise burrows on his belly with stretch of arm and using also the extension of tools designed for deep burrow probing. He rode up shotgun in the cab of heavy equipment, joking with the operators as they moved dirt around after areas had been judged clear of gopher tortoise presence. In his unforced but captivating manner, predicated on true interest and extra effort, he won the friendship and admiration of any and all with whom he worked.

Dan simply shook his head at all of it, in his customary, smiling manner, his spontaneous reaction to Delbert's magic that had impressed him for years.

The word of an organized python hunt in the Everglades reached Dan in late April, along with reaffirmation that he had been asked to participate in a yet undetermined capacity and had been trusted to bring along a competent guest, one who was well-suited for rough country travel and knew the ways and demands of wild Florida backcountry. Thusly, Delbert's candidacy was confirmed again without question.

Lily and Mae Ella were eager to make an official start on the exciting Delbert Turner retirement toast that was scheduled secretly for late October that year at the nature center in the Wahaweechee State Park that just happened to boast the name of their special honoree. They planned to launch into action in full earnest as soon as their hubbies left on their five-day python safari to south Florida. They were poised to hold their organizational meeting with other essential folks in order to get the whole secret process moving forward toward what they hoped would be an event that would resonate unforgettably in the minds of those present for their entire lives.

Dan planned to drive one of his *Real Florida Outdoors* vehicles with his company logo etched boldly across side doors and rear panels. Correctly, he reasoned that it never hurt to let the public know who they were and what they were about. Whenever he drove around his beloved state, he always tried to be motoring in a mobile billboard.

Repeatedly, over the years at his lecture gatherings, he had casually asked folks if they had seen any of his company vehicles out and about on Florida highways and motoring on secondary, backcountry roads. Many, many people answering in the affirmative were reasons enough to continue being noticed, so he continued the travel practice for years.

Delbert arrived at *Le Terrier de Renard* in his old Ford, very early on a Tuesday morning, ready for their departure. He was traveling light, as usual, carrying a small duffel bag only partially full with few changes of clothing and a battered Dopp kit containing essentials for teeth and face stubble and a used bar of soap wrapped in a paper towel. He carried a light, windbreaker jacket and wore a sweat-stained ballcap that Mae Ella had flat insisted upon running through the washer and dryer to keep clouds of insects from arriving in swarming convention mode.

It wasn't that Delbert was dirty and unkempt. He wasn't slovenly. He simply liked the same garb to wear until use and age literally disintegrated these favorite clothes. When a shirt, or a cap, or a pair of bluejeans finally died in tatters, it was like losing a member of his family. But, having them cleaned regularly was a plus he enjoyed. Delbert was not averse to getting slicked up in clean, well-worn duds, but he could get happily filthy with the best when tramping around in Florida woods during his diligent environmental rounds.

Delbert parked his rickety, old Ford out of the way, away from possible interference with the comings and goings of Lily and handyman, Fred. He looked for

Dan and found him at once, stowing his own travel gear in the gleaming Land Rover chosen for their trip.

He was not aware that Mae Ella had planned to arrive at *Le Terrier de Renard* within an hour of their departure so she and Lily could break new and fertile ground for the October toast extravaganza that was going to be huge, a celebration for the interesting, productive, and caring life of a certain Delbert Turner. At this point, the festive event remained a total surprise and Mae Ella and Lily were determined to keep it a secret until the very moment in October when someone yet unnamed delivered Delbert to his own celebration.

Dan and Delbert were away in moments. Delbert waved energetically at Lily standing on her front porch with both arms arching through the air. Dan blew kisses to her and nodded an answer to her special expression that telegraphed her firm wish for them to be totally alert and careful.

Sticking to the backcountry roads, Dan couldn't resist his ever-ready temptation to scout for roadkill retrieval, and going about that glum business, requiring starting and stopping, was just plain dangerous driving on the whisking interstates.

"When we get around gridlock Orlando, we'll be fine. A little out of our way now, avoiding heavy traffic, but a straight shot down to where we're going from Narcoossee south."

"How far all tolt?" asked Delbert.

"I ran a Mapquest on computer. Two hundred, twenty-one miles. We're not due until late this afternoon so let's kick back and enjoy the real Florida."

"Anytime we's in Florida backcountry, we's livin' real good," bellowed Delbert. "Boy, howdy," he exclaimed, slapping both his thighs.

"You got that right, partner."

"Where at we's a-stayin'?"

"They set up some wall tents, like the military use. They have bunks for everybody. Pretty rustic, but who cares. At least we're not sleeping out in the open, on the ground, even though this is the dry season. The wall tent will keep out the creepy crawlers so we don't wake up being kissed by some friendly moccasin or rattler."

"Or a gator," blurted Delbert. "Dem momma gators a-protectin' dem cute babies with dem yellow bands, right 'bout now."

"Say, you're right."

"Ain't never rassled no grown gator," joked Delbert. "Mebbe I oughta add dat to ma bucket list."

"You do, and Mae Ella will scalp me, Injun style, for letting you try. Now that's a fact. No gator wrestling, period!"

"Naw, too plum old," wearied Delbert.

"You're not too old, it just takes a while to learn the technique, even as fast as you learn things in the wild. Quicker than anyone I've ever known. But, we don't have the time for you to learn on this trip. We've got to concentrate on helping the guys going into the Glades, swamps and grasslands, as they try to capture some nasty pythons."

"Do you think me and you be behind dem front lines, so to speak, a-helpin' at a distance only, like me and you done dem times on dem wild fires?"

"I do indeed. We're support, not a couple of Tarzans. That's okay with you, right?"

"Sure 'nough is. We's seen plenty of action close to dem fires. Ma face hurt fer a week, likein' I been ta da beach from sun up ta sun down. Jes glad ta be a part of whatever dem dare folks say fer us to do."

"Good man. Good man. That's the spirit."

Out about an hour, Dan cruised by Narcoossee and Ashton and headed east toward Holopaw, where he made a sharp right, heading toward Kenansville, Yeehaw Junction, and then Fort Drum.

Critter roadkill was scarce, good news that pleased Dan. He stopped only twice the first hour, both armadillos, giving them each a decent burial off the shoulder of the road, with his energetic shovel digging shallow graves, but deep enough to fool the scent of vultures.

As they passed Forever Florida, a modest, country theme park with excellent food, a big-tire bus tour along bumpy, often wet, puddle roads leading alternately through high pine forests and scruffy Florida scrub, and a tourist zipline, a favorite for airborne enthusiasts, Dan mentioned what Lily and he had cooked up as a possible meeting place for the four of them at the end of their five-day adventure.

"You know all about what Lily was planning with Mae Ella? Both of them meeting down here at Forever Florida with us coming back up from the Glades, meeting for some great catfish. And taking two cars home from here. She mentioned all this to you, right?"

"Sure did. Heard all 'bout it. Good idée. But, can we's get cleaned up some, half decent, down dare after five days sweatin' and workin'?"

"Wow, you never used to worry about how you looked, or smelled for that matter, in the old days when I first knew you. Before . . . before, I repeat, before you got married."

Dan arched his eyebrows and flung a lopsided grin across his face.

Delbert blushed. A hint of faint red flushed across his well-worn, craggy features.

"You knowt them women folks. They likes you nice and clean for spoonin' and such."

"I know, ole buddy. Wasn't born yesterday, you know."

"Rekon we's will look likein' a couple of tramps!"

"No."

"No," replied Delbert hopefully.

"No, you will be a charmer, if you keep a clean change of clothes in reserve or wash some the last day."

"They set up for a-washin'?"

"Sure. This isn't going to be any five-star hotel deal, but they do have a water truck and makeshift showers. Kind of like safari-style in Africa. Modern day safari. We'll get showers. We'll be roughing it for sure, but we'll get showers. You don't mind cold water?"

"No . . . no. Cold fine. Then we's can get cleaned up?"

"Yes, Romeo. Honestly, Delbert, married life is agreeing with you. You ole smoothie, you."

"Dadburn super news. Dem ladies like usin' men smellin' good and lookin' clean after hard workin' outdoor stuff."

"You are right on, ole buddy. No worries. Who knows you might get a Hollywood offer as a leading man in the movies."

"Naw, Dan. Now youse pullin' my leg. I dumb, but not stupid."

"Quit that talk about being dumb. In your own way, uneducated with little schooling, with you going to work early to support your brothers and sisters, you're one of the most naturally smart persons I've ever known. Bar none."

"Aw, go on," denied Delbert.

"Take it or leave it. My compliment is sincere."

South of Kenansville, at the edge of the road itself, they encountered a roadkill hog, a big, black tusker.

"Killed right where he was, no doubt," said Dan, slowing the Land Rover. The presence of the silenced hog was visible from a quarter of a mile.

"Him done grown," whistled Delbert.

"What hit him has some real bumper or fender damage. Maybe both. He must weight three hundred, if he weighs an ounce. I don't think I can move him very easily, shovel or not. Besides, I'd be digging a grave until sundown and we need to keep moving. I'll call a buddy I know down in Yeehaw. Maybe we can set up some kind of closure for this poor giant through him."

Dan and Delbert, each with a tool, a shovel and an axe, pushed and pulled the dead weight of the hog off to the shoulder of the road.

"There. At least he won't get hit again, and maybe hurt somebody riding or driving. Not much solace in that with the damage done, but at least it's something."

Dan hated roadkill. He was silent for several miles, his thoughts a cauldron of upsetness.

Past Yeehaw, he resumed some semblance of his usual, sunny self.

"Do you know much about the Everglades, ole buddy?" asked Dan.

Delbert, who had been drinking in the wonderful Florida backcountry scenery, also while silent, replied, "Seen a bunch of pitchers. Mighty purdy country."

"Would you like some facts about where we are going? You know me, always butting in with some history lesson that almost everybody yawns over and then forgets."

They laughed together.

137

"Sure I would. This here old noggin gots plenty of empty space fer some wisdom. Am that da right word, 'wisdom'?"

"Sure, wisdom. Fits fine," smiled Dan.

"Put some wisdom on me then."

"Well, here goes. Take a nap if I ramble too long."

"No nap. Me scoutin' down some wisdom."

"First off, the true Everglades are a good bit larger than Everglades National Park, where we will be near at our destination today. Much larger! No little chunk of earth, the national park, mind you, but only a part of the extensive Everglades themselves. The national park itself is 1.5 million acres. That's roughly four percent of the land in Florida. It was set aside in 1948, as Florida's first national park. President Truman did the honors when the park opened, the ribbon-cutting ceremony and such. By the way, I might mention, Florida has two other national parks, Dry Tortugas off Key West and Biscayne, south of Miami."

"Bet many folks in da dark 'bout dem other two," offered Delbert.

"Right you are. Many folks think just Everglades. Amazing. It was a long fight getting it set aside by the dedicated persistence of many people. Over time! Really, it was on the verge of taking place before World War II, but it all came together short years afterward. Many people, building upon the work of others and striving forward with new push ideas of their own. That's really how most great things come into being, or how inventions arrive, for that matter. Building blocks through time hoisted from shoulder to shoulder, so to speak. Got me so far? You're not dozing off?"

"Not me. Me a-miss too much wisdom coming up. Naw! Got ma arms 'round what you been asayin'. Ain't got no toothpicks holdin' my eyes open. Spoon me out a new bowl of dat wisdom."

"Good. I'll wear my professor hat a little bit longer then."

"Darn tootin'."

"Probably the most influential person in the historical mix of the Everglades story was a lady named Marjorie Stoneman Douglas. She was a newspaper journalist, writer, and a huge activist for all things environmental. Like you! And, get this, she lived to be 108 years old, living through the terms of 21 presidents, from Benjamin Harrison, when she was born in 1890, until Bill Clinton, when she passed in 1998."

"Jumpin' spiders," exclaimed Delbert. "She musta had some doctor note for some powerful vitamins orin the good Lord done put her here for a heap of good works. Dat took some time ta do."

"Maybe a little of both," laughed Dan. "Eight years old during the Spanish-American War and lived nearly to the 21st Century. Just imagine what she saw in her lifetime. Born thirteen years before the Wright Brothers at Kitty Hawk."

"She could tell some stories. Now that a fact," nodded Delbert vigorously.

"When she died, she had lived almost exactly half the actual time we were a country. Unreal! She wrote about the environment and its desperate cry for protection and care. Her famous book, *The River of Grass*, about the Everglades, had a tremendous impact everywhere. And, she was a gifted speaker too, preaching, preaching, preaching about protecting the Everglades at town meetings, public gatherings, anywhere and everywhere."

"What a lady," Delbert shook his head up and down the whole time Dan was speaking.

139

"I memorized one of her famous quotes, as we talk about her and her wonderful accomplishments at *Real Florida Outdoors* sometimes. She said this:"

There are no other Everglades in the world. They are, they always have been, one of the unique regions of the earth, remote and not wholly known. Nothing anywhere else is like them.

"Me, I step down offin' the sidewalk inta da gutter ta let her past," saluted Delbert.

"Isn't it so," smiled Dan at Delbert's homespun tribute.

They drifted silent for several miles, continuing to drink in the semi-tropical vista unfolding along the eastern shore of Lake Okeechobee, that was broken with large tracks of cultivated farmland. Dan spiced their interlude of curiosity with mention of the famous battle on Christmas Day, 1837, during the Second Seminole War, which was the prominent war of three fought in Florida in the 19th Century between the Seminoles and the U.S Army.

"Colonel Taylor, he was in 1837, not yet a general. Zackary Taylor, who went on to great military success in the Mexican War a few years later and, after than, the Presidency, won in 1848. He became our 12th President but didn't live through his term. He engaged Seminoles, hiding behind trees and hidden in long grass near Lake Okeechobee here. Colonel Taylor lost many more soldiers to death and wounds than the casualties suffered by the poor Seminoles, who fled the field of battle in stashed canoes, paddling out and away into the big lake, when they had inflicted as much damage as they thought possible. Clearly, the Seminoles had won the battle.

However, Delbert, the chore of reporting the outcome of the battle fell to Colonel Taylor, and in his report to Congress and the War Department, he said, and I quote for you a part, *'The Seminoles fled in every direction'."*

"Well, the powers in Washington bought his assessment, he had been clobbering Native Americans since 1808 by the way, and they honored him by promoting him to General. So much for historical accuracy in the annals of American history."

"No foolin'?" asked Delbert, haltingly.

"No fooling," repeated Dan, opening both his hands on the steering wheel in a quizzical gesture.

Well past Belle Glade and starting the final fifty, bumpy mile push to their rendezvous with the python hunt organizers and participants, Dan hesitantly asked Delbert a question.

"Have you heard me blabber on enough about the Everglades and Florida history, or could you endure one final topic on this drive down, that is the python problem itself. I wouldn't mind one bit if you said you were going to take a shotgun seat nap and would I please shut-up!"

"I ain't tired none if you's a-talkin'. Me listenin' hard and learnin' some real wisdom. Keep on a-talkin'. Me a-tryin' ta educate my lone self all I cans."

"Okay. If you're sure."

"Plumb, real sure."

"Okay. We have nearly an hour to go. I'll wear myself out beating my gums if you want to listen."

"Wants to."

"Have you heard the term 'exotic plants and animals'?"

141

"Sure have. Dems is plants and animals dat don't belongs none in Florida. Dem come in here, invadin' like folks say."

"Good job," approved Dan. "The word 'exotic' dictionary style, literally means 'foreign or imported.' Another meaning is 'having charm or fascination.' And, a third definition is 'strangely beautiful or enticing.' Those are dictionary definitions, word for word, not mine. We have, today in Florida, many of these 'exotics," brought here for sale, mostly, in the case of animals, as so-called 'exotic pets,' intended to be the source of traditional, cultural medicines, or even as eventual culinary delicacies. The exotic plant world is a wholly different area, and I won't touch on it here, even though its impact is huge."

"Understand," added Delbert. "Likein' hyacinth and hydrilla."

"Yes," brightened Dan, almost amazed at the little gems of knowledge Delbert did, in fact, know.

"Well, you know people, right? Some people collect these exotic animals as bragging rights, or simply because they like to show off and be talked about."

Delbert nodded, intent on hearing more.

"Well, a brisk, lucrative trafficking with exotic animals developed in Florida over the years. People buying imported animals when they were small and cute. Lizards, snakes, tropical fish, others. A huge business emerged and flourished. And then, guess what happened?"

"Dem little critters got all growed up and dem critters gots too big to be safe like and too much on da poor pocketbook ta keep a-feedin' and a-carin' for."

"Exactly. And then what?"

"Folks went to a-cartin' dem critters outa lonely roads outa town and lettin' 'em go inta da wild places not far from people places."

"Exactly again, Delbert. Exactly."

"Yup."

"And then what?"

"Trouble."

"Exactly, a third time. And, that brings us to Burmese pythons, the reason we're on the road today. The first Burmese python, originally from Southeast Asia, was discovered in the Everglades in 1979. It was removed and no more reported until 1995. More than a coincidence after Hurricane Andrew in 1992. There were reports of some of these scary reptilian boys and girls escaping to the wild from damaged buildings as a result of that hurricane. But, since 2000, these big, constrictor snakes, those that kill by squeezing, have exploded in numbers. Several hundred of them have been identified as being inside Everglades National Park. The actual number is undoubtedly higher. They are breeding, no question! Many, many pitched there by bored owners, or frightened owners, or owners, as you say, feeling it in the pocketbook when it comes to feeding them. Some seen have been fifteen feet long and they can grow to nineteen feet and weigh over two hundred pounds."

"Big, bad boys," added Delbert.

"For certain. Now, I don't want to stretch the truth. Let's be fair. Pythons don't slither around, searching for humans as prey. They don't stalk folks. However, as a sit-and-wait, opportunistic predator, they certainly can kill a human, and wouldn't hesitate if one got directly in their way."

"No foolin'! Flat true," agreed Delbert.

"These pythons are now the apex predator in the Everglades. They are very resilient. Once released, they are quite expert at finding food, water, shelter. And, in only a matter of time, they find mates. Young pythons with umbilical cord scars have been found and captured, proving these former sweetheart pets now breed in the wild."

"Worries a bunch," chimed Delbert.

"Yes. No question. There is great deal of worry about the python impact on native Everglades species. We already know a lot and fear more. Stomach contents of roadkill and captured pythons have revealed that they eat small mammals here, rabbits, squirrels, even possums and raccoons. And we fear for our birdlife, because, in their native range thousands of miles away, they tend to camp in wait around wading bird roosts and actually climb trees at night to prey on them. They may make our birds prey candidates, like the limpkins, which are not accustomed to defending themselves from nocturnal predators."

"Bad, bad," wagged Delbert, as he slid a calloused hand down the length of his craggy face.

"The fish and water commission is trying all kinds of things to get this growing problem under control. Authorizing its officers to kill them on lands they manage, starting tag programs on captured pythons, hopeful that radio-tracking devices might reveal patterns and information that would enhance capture in the future. And, they are pushing for stricter penalties to fight the practice of illegal abandonment. Also, appealing to pet shops to take back unwanted larger snakes previously purchased directly from them. They also want exotic animal control and funding for it to host a congressional goal to recharge and cleanse the Everglades."

"Folks a-workin'."

"Yes, they are. From many sides. Hopefully, smarter humans can win over less smart reptiles, but one has to give them credit, they have been around longer than we have. That's a sobering thought when you stop and think. Whew! Maybe I'll stop there. I can feel my blood pressure rising."

"One more thing," gloomed Delbert, looking out his window, a furrowed study in concern.

"Shoot!"

"Hope a handle come on all this 'fore some tourist kids run inta python attacks dat end bad."

"Truer words never spoken," whistled Dan, with wide-eyed solemnity.

"Kiss goodbye a lot of dat tourist dollar ifin dat happen."

"Time to change the subject. Your truth cuts deep."

Dan and Delbert arrived at their camp destination late in the afternoon, driving most of an entire day, that was punctuated by six roadkill episodes and three comfort stops that doubled as coffee refreshment time. Their trip had been unhurried, a design that matched their early departure. Delicious sandwiches prepared by Lily and Mae Ella, nestled in their iced coolers, made restaurants unnecessary along their way.

Dan's first impression, as he surveyed the camp site when they parked, was the thought that if Florida sported safaris like Africa with their camera or rifle adventures, they must look similar to the view that bore his inspection.

The site was remote, that was a given and no surprise. But, the actual location, at the end of a 14-mile bone-jarring, jerking carnival ride for vehicles over a sand-rutted ribbon of road looked like a postcard candidate for statewide ecotourism billboards that would have caught the eye of any and every traveling motorist.

There was a huddle of lazy sabal palms, weighted with drooping brown fronds rasping in the gentle breeze, but the palms also boasted green fronds, quite alive and blowing quietly in the same gentle breeze. The late April sun was aslant, sinking in the west, warm and prominent against a blue sky, virtually devoid of clouds. The weather was supposed to cooperate for their hunt, the local meteorologists had bragged. The odds favored their prediction, as the dry season, if history were to be an indicator, was locked in for several weeks.

The campsite, about the size of a basketball court, was practically barren, almost absent of even short grass, as though it had been mowed regularly, even though that never was the case. In the middle of the clearing sat a fire ring, surrounded by a mixture of folding, camp chairs. A fresh cone of firewood sat arranged in a flue perfect creation, a perfect pile of dry kindling and stout logs just begging for a lit match at nightfall so a bright, crackling fire would add suspense to the strategy talk that was certain to be staged by the leaders running the hunt.

Five wall tents, wearing military camouflage as loose sweaters, sat in a semi-circular arc well up and away from surrounding Everglades water that was barely moving amid stands of thick grass. Four powerful airboats rested eerily still at the edge of the slightly inclined bank leading up from the vast sheet of quiet water. The airboats were moored by strong ropes tied in complicated navy knots to the stoutest palms. Two Port-O-Lets, a water truck with a nearby curtained, outdoor shower, and a makeshift, portable kitchen with awning completed the temporary sights at their camp city.

Most of the men were young and extremely fit, the type who relished dangerous tussles with alligators and big snakes. Dan wasn't disappointed at all. He, like Delbert, had experienced his time in the wild arena, with its most contentious moments, and he was happy to beg off hands-on warfare with bacteria-laden reptiles, content to substitute instead what he hoped would be worthwhile cerebral decisions and all types of liaison support when needed and asked.

"Plenty of young warriors to go one-on-one with pythons here among us. We're support back-up only, that's obvious," cracked Dan with a sideways whisper.

"Lookee like it, don't it," agreed Delbert. "Aint no problem no way. Jes bein' glad a-bein' here."

"Right on. We'll look busy and stay busy."

"What you call it, anti . . ., anti . . ., uh . . ., anticipate what a-needs doin'."

"Exactly."

Dan knew about one-third of the twenty or so of the men gathered, mostly the older coots, like Delbert and himself. They weren't snubbed, not at all. Their own solid reputations for things accomplished outdoors had arrived ahead of them in the minds of many. They were welcomed warmly with smiling nods and steady handshakes, and thereby immediately put at ease, feeling needed and wanted by all who introduced themselves.

The cook shack began to radiate some decent aromas along about sunset and the cone of fueled firewood, drywood helping, sprung to crackling life in a matter of minutes. Men drifted out of their walled tents and claimed vacant chairs that quickly formed a complete circle around the orange-red fire. The sharp smell of cigar smoke wafted across the clearing. And, the sound of laughter and convivial conversation happily broke the primeval silence normally occasioning the evening solitude at this remote eastern Everglades campsite.

Hamburger steak, deli potato salad and baked beans prepared first thirty miles away in Miami and driven to the campsite, and traditional south Florida key lime pie filled a host of appreciative stomachs. There would be food shuttle every day to the campsite bringing fresh, refrigerated meals for preparation on site. Hunt rules, to which all had agreed previously, forbade alcoholic beverages anywhere during the four and a half-day hunt. Of course, many of the men normally enjoyed their beers and bourbon, but no complaints were registered at dinner. Everyone seemed to realize the importance of what they were trying to accomplish, understanding the danger of it, a concerted approach against nasty pythons, best served by no booze distractions.

After dinner, everyone policed their own trash, depositing Styrofoam containers and plastic silverware in lined barrels. Then, they returned to their circle of folding chairs around the fading fire that was beginning to hiss and crackle toward its ember death. The leader of the hunt, a state official whom Dan had known for years, outlined his working plan for hopeful success, while standing before his team seated around the darkening fire.

Everyone received an individual assignment, designed to make the entire team operate smoothly and efficiently. Their leader announced that they would assess progress every night around a fire, tweaking things democratically by vote in an attempt to improve ongoing success. He explained that his opening plan for the first day was intended to form a baseline, saying that a start idea needed to be in place. However, he reiterated his awareness that they were all professionals and that he respected that happy circumstance and that he had no intent to bully things in any pushy, dictatorial manner, beyond trying to establish guidance for their goals.

Dan was asked to take lengthy notes during the hunt and further asked to produce and issue a complete report once the hunt was over. He agreed heartily, telling everyone how much he appreciated their confidence . Delbert was assigned the up close task of measuring and weighing euthanized pythons after capture, hunt parlance for tabulating python results with a footstick by which success or failure was gauged.

Both Dan and Delbert shared ice chest and cooler duty aboard their airboats, a stock and carry chore shared by many. It was late April and growing seasonally warm, days in the mid 80's and nights nudging down only to the mid 60's. Staying hydrated with steady intake of liquids would be vital. Dan and Delbert were assigned to different airboats, and they would be with different teams each day on different airboats, in an effort to maximize coordinated contact and camaraderie with everyone in the group.

Everyone trooped off to their bunks, feeling upbeat about the meeting that had been conducted with a positive tone. The fire was kicked to a state of no remaining life and then dowsed with a bucket of water. Night watch assignments were drawn, not that anyone was expecting any attack from either animal or human.

A coordinated night watch added purpose to their important and serious adventure. Everyone understood. Dan drew an early watch, ten o'clock to midnight. Delbert, with no luck coming his way, claimed the last watch before dawn, the tough one for a good night sleep. They both would be free from night watch duty the second night, but would return to the same rotation schedule the third night.

Excitement reigned in camp as everyone fought the temptation to talk away the night. Eventually, the team settled down for sleep, enthused as a bunch of school kids going to a next day carnival. Truly, the python hunt team was billeted in remote south Florida backcountry. Stars above were their electric lights,

149

and those stars sparkled in prominence the first night, too many perhaps for even a computer to count, ablaze overhead, a still and windless night, totally without cloud cover.

CHAPTER VIII

The success of the python hunt was found in the renewed awareness of the exotic animal and plant problems in Florida, as the hunt, conducted without specifically naming location or the parties participating, was covered well by the print and video media. In addition, it also spawned a number of new, collateral articles and television news spots that chronicled both the exotic animal invasion directly threatening humans and their pets as well as projecting a sharp refocus on the non-native plant invasion that had become on ongoing problem and a huge eradication expense in Florida for many decades.

Unfortunately, the results from the actual hunt were dismal, with no fault for the outcome assigned to the dedicated hunters, who worked diligently together at their purpose throughout the four and a half-day struggle that produced long, bone-weary hours with a total command effort.

Simply, the number of pythons found, captured and either euthanized or radio-collared to benefit future

151

research, was pitifully small. Either the pythons were slick at hiding well or the hunters had been telegraphing their trespass. Those were the two main riddles that the group beat to verbal death around the campfire each night.

The group voted down, without any actual show of hands, any notion that the loud airboats had chased the big snakes away from their hunt zone because the airboats, although gratingly noisy, were only used to shuttle all of them to dry land areas that pythons favored. Pythons traveled far less through water than their presence on land during their wanderings.

In addition, the airboat routes followed different directions, water paths used for speed to hunt destinations. Any travel noise was dispersed everywhere, not concentrated in one direction. Also, the hunt zones the group had picked were two miles from the silencing of the arriving airboats, allowing the raucous noise that reached the search area to return to a quieter normalcy.

Basically, the frustrated group of python hunters chalked up their glum results to simply hunter's bad luck. Most of them in the virtually hand-picked group had spent many years hunting in the Florida backcountry and they well knew that sometimes even the best-intentioned and best-planned hunts turned up very little or nothing at all.

Shrugging and smiling wanly, everyone readied to disperse and go their separate ways, hopeful that some data from their spirited wanderings, sloshing through water and trooping through stands of thick, slapping grasses would translate to better python hunting when the next organized hunt was scheduled. They didn't feel jinxed, just disappointed, as the final results were so scant.

Only five pythons had been found and euthanized. Twenty-seven feet, stretched end to end was the tally, with the longest python measuring only a little over eight feet in length. Delbert could have used a yardstick with his measuring chores instead of being outfitted with a fifty-yard tape measure.

On the morning of the fifth and final day of the forlorn hunt, Dan stayed in camp to organize his many notes, while the experience memories were still fresh in his mind. He would send a final, formal report from his home office within a week to his friend, the team leader. Delbert went out on an airboat one last time with one of the persistent teams, helping as usual with his gameface on, demonstrating the good attitude that had been his personal calling card for years.

By noon of the fifth day, vehicles billowing dust behind them into the air down the bumpy, washboard road, began to arrive from destinations unknown in the outside world to pick up many of the hunters. Only a few in the group, like Dan and Delbert, had come to the campsite in a vehicle that stayed parked the five days. Among the arriving lifelines to civilization was yet another newsvan from Miami that everyone tried to avoid, knowing that any interview would assign to anyone questioned the label of hunt failure, a scar that would be grossly unfair as all the assessment of the hunt had not been weighed and analyzed, and what might appear as failure, could, upon future determination, really turn out to be an innovative platform for the future.

Dan and Delbert were packed, and on the dusty road headed north before one o'clock, after a series of high-five salutes were passed all around to everyone with whom they had grown close, like soldiers becoming brothers in a wartime battle. They both had taken the last of the cold showers that morning and had dressed into somewhat clean field gear that had been washed in the "river of grass" itself and spread on grassy ground to dry in the sun. But no razor had fought a tussle with their faces for nearly a week. They laughed when Dan asked Delbert if he thought Mae Ella and Lily would recognize them.

As soon as a clear cell phone signal became available, Dan tapped Lily on his speed dial, and after gushy but heartfelt pronouncements of love to her were expressed, they confirmed their dinner plan at Forever Florida that the four of them had named as their reunion site after the five day separation.

"Mae Ella is already here. We're ready to leave. You said our driving time down would be about an hour and a quarter, is that right, honey?" questioned Lily.

"Yes. Very close to that," agreed Dan.

"Check."

"We're two hours and twenty minutes or so coming north. I ran a watch on it coming down, backing out three stops. Plenty of gas for us all the way."

"Two hours and twenty minutes. Good grief, you're as precise as a Cape landing."

Dan laughed into his cell phone.

"Then, if we leave in an hour, we'll arrive about together. I was terrible at math."

Tongue in cheek, just to tease, Dan said, "Oh, we may be off seven or eight minutes."

"You stinker!"

Again Dan laughed.

"We'll catch you up on all the python news at dinner. Or, should I say, the lack of python news."

"That bad?"

"In a way, that bad. But, maybe positive fallout to come. Hopeful."

"Change the subject," pressed Lily. "Can you answer just 'yes' or 'no'?"

"About what?"

"Silly, with Delbert sitting next to you, can you answer just 'yes' or 'no', if I talk about a certain thing?"

"Oh, yes. Yes."

"Come in world. Honestly. News flash, world to Dan. World to Dan."

"Yes."

"We won't breathe a word, not a word, with the four of us together at dinner. Mae Ella and I will be like statues. Stone statues on the secret subject."

"Yes. Yes."

"Good boy. Well, I can happily report that Mae Ella and I accomplished a lot. I mean a lot of details, and some real finalized plans as well. The works."

"Yes."

"You better say 'no' once for drill before we hang up, so he won't be suspicious and ask any questions."

"Uh, no. No. I mean yes."

"Super, I guess. You follow instructions well when you deal in monosyllabic nonsense," barbed Lily.

"Yes."

Now Lily laughed.

"How do you look?" she guardedly inquired.

"Horrible. Field gear we're wearing hand-washed with liquid kitchen soap and creek water. Sun-dried on the ground."

"Ugh. I was afraid to ask how you both look."

"Like some of the old war movies, black-and-white, we saw as kids."

"No injuries? You're fine, right?"

"Yes."

"You scared me."

"Sorry. Let's see, how do we look? Well, sandpaper faces. No razor. Five o'clock shadow building for five days, for starters."

"Oh, peachy keen. Mae Ella and I will sit at a different table at Forever Florida."

"Aw, babe," pined Dan.

"Just kidding. Just kidding."

"That wouldn't be any way to treat two returning conquering heroes!"

"Oh, brother. Listen to that. You better go back to simple 'yes' or 'no'."

Although Dan and Lily called each other several times as they both pointed toward their dinner rendezvous, Dan to report two additional roadkill retrieval delays, and Lily to direct additional "yes" and "no" duologues, brimming with exciting news about accomplishments Mae Ella and she had completed for Delbert's roast and toast extravaganza in October, their arrival time was near perfect, without either party speeding or slowing. Three minutes apart was their synchronized result.

They parked alongside each other, Dan and Delbert arriving last, and arm in arm, with smiles and laughter abounding, they walked into the Forever Florida Restaurant.

Dan had that glint in his eye, but reined back any outward enthusiasm with dear friends so close. Lily read him like a favorite book.

"Shave first when we get home," she whispered coyly in her easy way of placing simple and easily overcome obstacles before mutually desired intimacy.

Mae Ella and Delbert embraced as if he had been absent for years, fighting in some foreign war. Lily and Dan glowed at their way of still showing their deep love for each other after several years of marriage.

156

Ordering dinner was a mimic all around, without even consult of menu. Four catfish dinners with French fries, coleslaw, and hush puppies sounded so good when Mae Ella floated her food desire to their waiter, the others chimed in their agreement with eager nods. When the beverage of choice was suggested, Mae Ella led the charge toward aroma heaven accompaniment with her request for unsweetened iced tea and the others clamored to agree. The surprised waiter was at their table under a minute, a sure signal that the folks at his table station were ravenously hungry. Actually, they all had feasted on fried catfish before at Forever Florida and no one had even remotely considered an alternative. The young waiter sped to the kitchen with their order, the grin across his face telegraphing without words the wish that dealing with all customers should be this smooth.

Conversation at early dinner, about four in the afternoon, with lunch skipped by everyone, in order to savor their feast, was limited to a reluctant replay of the python hunt. Mae Ella and Lily couldn't utter a syllable about what they had been secretly doing all week, so they asked a Gatling gun of questions, one after another, trying to get the boys to relate every detail of their python experience.

A very subtle but familiar facial cue from Delbert to Dan deftly passed that ticklish subject over to him. He could have won an Oscar with its portrayal had Hollywood offered such an award in the dubious category of nonsense amplification.

After the offering of a series of short, fuzzy answers, Dan delivered a vague, vapid dud that would have left any crowd speechless, if not vomiting.

"We await time and accurate results going forward in the area of data interpretation with the cooperative desire of everyone to allow our field findings to form a kind of benchmark for future

157

investigations that will heighten the retention and capture capability of these beautifully-marked but potentially dangerous snakes indigenous to lands far away."

Lily looked down at the bottom of her slacks and the top of her sandals afraid some restroom commode had overflowed on the premises and flush water was running apace throughout their restaurant area.

"What python success did you have during those five long days?" sampled Mae Ella. "I'll bet you saw an awful lot."

"Well, as I just said, all the data evaluation will be forthcoming, hopefully in the form of very tangible results, down the road so to speak."

"Oh," managed Mae Ella, staring down at her plate of catfish bones.

Lily sensed Dan's awkward gist of conversation emerging and she sought to steer away from any further agony, at least until they could talk alone going home.

"We are crying for rain at home. I know it's the dry season, but we are hurting. Dry! Dry! Dry! Did you get much rain in the Glades?"

Dan savored his escape opportunity to change the subject, jumping right into the old, time-honored weather topic with both feet.

"Sprinkled one evening, isn't that right, Delbert? Only a teaser rain though."

"Ain't 'nough to wet a frog's lips. Heared it on top to ourin tent, and plumb over 'afore a soul coulda step out ta see ifin a drop might hit him."

The catfish dinner with all the trimmings was delicious as always. True to ordering sequence, all four passed on dessert, partly because they were watching their waistlines, but mostly because both couples were in a hurry to return to the comfort of home where Delbert and Dan could wash away the rest of the trail dust and grime with bar soap and hot water.

On the road again they were, headed north, destinations eastern Seminole County for Lily and Dan, and coastline Brevard County for Mae Ella and Delbert.

Lily patted Dan's right shoulder, lingering her hand there, as they began the journey home. Mae Ella and Delbert drove behind them.

"It was only five days, honey, but I'm so glad you're back. I missed you terribly, just want you to know."

"Nice words and I know you mean them. That makes them nicer."

"All true."

Dan winked, smiled, and fashioned a kiss sound across to her.

"You know, I never cease to wonder at your uncanny ability to deflect things with words when it is essential to explain away a delicate situation. Amazing, utterly amazing."

"Oh, you mean back there at the dinner table," smirked Dan.

"Yes, of course."

"I knew that you knew what I was doing."

"Of course."

"Practicing."

"Of course."

"Hated to use dear friends like Delbert and Mae Ella as captive guinea pigs."

"I know, but you were running through what you will be forced to say everywhere in defense of an unsuccessful python hunt. You were practicing."

"Yes, but much of my rehearsed comments may be quite true. Actually so."

"True," nodded Lily.

"Everyone at the offices will be asking all about it. Asking the boss, putting him on the spot. Big time!"

"And, if you talk in a scientific vein, not lying, just scientifically, you don't have to make all kinds of personal excuses for a poor python adventure that wasn't your fault."

"Yes, exactly. I'm not embarrassed about it. I'm not ashamed of it. But, given the bully pulpit which falls my way, I can be positive and take the high ground."

"And you should. You won't lie outright, just stress the positives that build for the future.

"Couldn't say it better myself."

"Settled. Done."

"Tell me about Humphrey. How's he been? And then I want to hear about all the success you and Mae Ella had with the plans for Delbert's big day in October."

"Humphrey's fine. Typical sweet Maltese. Knows when we both leave and gets sad. He looked for you every late afternoon, running to the front door and barking. Then he goes to our low front windows where he can see out and looks anxiously down the driveway, looking back at me with hope for your return etched across his darling face."

"That sweetheart. He's God's love on earth."

"Precious, precious," murmured Lily.

"I'll see that little champ in less than an hour, can't wait."

"Oh, I know you love him dearly."

"Dearly! Shoot on the Delbert development. Tell me. Tell me."

"Where to start? We arranged so much. Let's see, start at the beginning, Lily ole gal."

"Can't wait to hear."

160

"First things first. We made sure, double sure, that October 26th, all day, and the day before, the 25th, were reserved for us alone. The 25th for decorations, and some of us arriving with some of the refrigerated foods ahead of time. For those two big commercial refrigerators at the nature center."

"No school field trips? No scout merit badge outings? No senior citizens, with bus visits from retirement centers?" coached Dan.

"Nothing. Clean as a whistle for us. Both days."

"You must have talked with the decision-making folks. State park honchos."

"Yes. We got the right names and called those decision folks. Got it from the horse's mouth, as they say. Two different confirmations. The right kind of backup. Of course, they knew all about Delbert. I even asked politely for a short letter from them to confirm further. The Delbert Turner Nature Center in Wahaweechee is reserved. And, everyone with whom we spoke swore to strict secrecy."

"And, of course, you'll touch base again long about the end of August, or first of September."

"Already planned. Marked on two different calendars."

"Good. The firm reservation, time and place, is the biggee."

"Mae Ella and I called chair rental places and we were offered some good deals. They have tables too. Can reserve plenty of both, but thought maybe our own *Real Florida Outdoors* may want to loan the chairs. You have plenty. We told them we would finalize this week with them after I've talked with you."

"We can do chairs and tables. Both! We're happy to solve that request. Can do. I'll have tables shuttled over to Sanford headquarters as we draw close

161

and we'll gather folding Samsonite chairs from all seven locations as well as we draw close to event time. And, babe, we'll deliver too, all the tables and chairs in plenty of time for you ladies and your helpers to set up and decorate without being rushed."

"I knew you would. Super."

"Any thoughts yet on meal goodies, who will get invitations, what you are going to charge, and any arrangements on background music, live or a good sound system?"

"Wow, you're a regular task master!"

"Probably too early for all that," backed off Dan.

"No, I told you Mae Ella and I were busy. We're up to speed, buster. Answers for everything you mentioned."

"Wow, that is impressive."

"Early thoughts on the lunch menu, are as follows, Mr. Miller!"

"Dan, simply Dan, is acceptable," he joked.

"Fried chicken, pulled pork, sweet potatoes, corn on the cob, collards, baked beans, cheese grits, swamp cabbage, cooked fresh and hot, *not* hearts of palm canned, hushpuppies, coleslaw, pimento-cheese filled celery, okra, buttermilk biscuits, homemade ice cream, peach cobbler, and key lime pie."

"Wish it were tomorrow. Wow! A banquet!"

"And drinks. Sweet tea, lemonade, soft drinks, all types."

"Bottled water too?"

"That's a given, yes. Okay, invitations from the governor on down. Some members of his cabinet. Both U.S senators, local state legislators, local county officials, state fish and wildlife folks, the people where Delbert cast his special spell over the years, like, for example, the ancient canoe folks, the thankful forest fire folks, the emu rancher where Delbert captured the runaway emu. Many, many others he touched with his magical skills over the years. We really made quite a list because Delbert made few friends but touched so many lives. Of course, no invitations have been sent at this point, only our list for later mailing."

"Shyness. He made few close friends because he was a secretive loner and so wonderfully modest. But, those he did touch with his magical skills in the woods became lifetime admirers."

"Of course. We spread the invitation blanket wide."

"George and Clara Mason? Duffy and his wife, Edna? Henry Sullivan and his inner circle?"

"No worries. They were placed on the list first."

"How many names so far?"

"One hundred and fifteen."

"H'mm. A good number, I'll wager. Eighty percent will attend," asserted Dan confidently.

"That was close to my estimate too," agreed Lily.

"Great minds, right?" teased Dan.

"Right. We haven't decided what to charge yet. We'll put a sharp pencil to it, ask for advice in that process, and hopefully have a fair amount chosen that we can place with the invitations going out."

"And, stress, placed on the invitation somewhere, big and bold letters, that all the proceeds go to the nature center for project development and such, and not as a love offering to Delbert and Mae Ella."

"That will be made abundantly clear. Yes."

"Smart! You have time on this. You'll want them out not too soon or too late."

"Music. You mentioned music. Good news there too. We have bluegrass pickers committed.

Guitars and banjo. Even a country and western singer or two. Sound systems found too. Microphones also."

"Wow!"

"Pretty good for one week on the telephone, two gals making a long list of personal calls, and not actually mentioning Delbert's name once. We kept it as big a secret as Disney coming to the Orlando area."

"I would say marvelous if I had to pick a word," beamed Dan. "Simply marvelous."

"Oh, you just want a quick shave and a hot shower so you can get dirty and messed up all over again. I'm wise to you."

"Well . . . I've never said you weren't observant," replied Dan dryly with a certain gleam in his eye.

Resting with hot coffee mugs on their back porch the following morning, watching their dear white fluffball Humphrey chase his toys and a small parade of wildlife critters prance past their backyard pond, Lily smiled over at her husband.

"Do you have enough energy to go to the office, or do you need to spend the day at home?"

"Office! Office!" pled Dan, laughing aloud.

"Okay, if you say so, buster. But if I hear of any complaining, I want you to come directly home, that's an order."

"No complaining! No complaining! Office! Office!"

"Okay, are you sure?"

"Positive. Sure. Positive."

"Fine."

Dan sighed relief and had Lily laughing with him. They watched Humphrey and his cute antics, and then Lily spoke.

"So, what's on your upcoming agenda? There always is something brewing to flame your interest whenever one of your adventures, like the python hunt, turns out a little disappointing . You don't stay down long, you have too much fire in the belly."

"You know me pretty well. You're spot on. And, say thank you for the 'fire in the belly' compliment. Very nice."

"All true and proud to say it."

"Yes, I am excited about a new adventure I just put together in my mind early this morning. Boom, it shot right into my mind. I almost cheered out loud."

"Let's hear it."

"Do you remember, years ago, when the poor dusky seaside sparrow was going extinct over Merritt Island way?"

"Yes."

"Biologists were trying desperately to match up even one mating pair."

"Yes, I remember well."

"Loss of habitat, drainage of some scant remaining habitat too, zipping interstates, pesticides, Cape buildup and commotion, and all of a sudden, presto, where is that little guy, and then, the worst case scenario, the dusky seaside sparrow was no more. Gone! Finished! History! Extinct as in Forever."

"Sad, so sad. Sad beyond words."

"Well, guess what! We have that same glum picture show trying to run again downstate. That train to nowhere picture show with possible extinction as the last empty station on the route."

"Oh, no! Where and what blessed creature?"

"A little sparrow called the 'grasshopper sparrow.' Tiny! Maybe five inches long and weighing maybe an ounce. Mostly gray and black with brown streaks on its back. Underneath, light gray. At the bend of its wings, bright yellow, and the little guy sports an orange patch in front of its eyes and a white stripe on its head."

"Called the grasshopper sparrow?" quizzed Lily.

"Yes. Its song is so weak and like a grass hopper sound, thus the name."

"Afraid to ask. Petrified to ask."

Dan waited.

"Is . . . is, . . . is the end game as near as was the sad situation with the dusky seaside?" measured Lily, drawing up her pretty mouth into a wince, awaiting perhaps an answer she greatly feared.

"No," pronounced Dan. "Not quite yet."

"Hooray," cheered Lily, "maybe we can win this one."

Humphrey, startled, barked at her exuberance.

"Maybe," cautioned Dan. "It can still be identified in the wild, but only in a few places, in Osceola, Polk, Highlands, and Okeechobee counties. They lately have been seen in only seven occupied locations, all within thirty miles of each other. Authorities at the Fish and Game Wildlife Conservation Commission and the state park service are combining efforts to start a captive breeding program, a concerted effort, with the help of volunteer spotters, like us, to collect eggs so that they can whisk them over to the Rare Species Conservancy in Loxahatchee, down near West Palm Beach."

"Us! Us!"

"Oh, yes, honey, I didn't tell you. All of this is so new, just leaping into my head as clear as a bell, just hours ago. I plan to volunteer some time as a spotter, and I'm excited enough to take Delbert, George, and Duffy in a Land Rover to donate some volunteer bird-finding. I'm getting right on it this morning. I'll get them to commit to two days at least. I'll make it happen."

"Can they get away? I mean, Duffy and George!"

166

"I'll make it happen. Delbert will go. Duffy has two sons now at the restaurant. And, Clara and a college boy or two can run Otter Creek for a couple of days. I'm on a mission. I'll make it happen."

Lily processed Dan's surprise quickly, knowing exactly what is was, partly pure passion for the beleaguered grasshopper sparrow and partly hopeful retribution for a disappointed snake hunt. Having no secrets from her husband, she fortified her gathering thoughts, in a clear statement to him.

"I salute your passion for the grasshopper sparrow. You earnestly and passionately want to help. Laudatory!'

"Thank you."

"I also know, and what I'm about to say is equally valid, knowing you so well, that you want a quick but genuine success to your credit so you can rally emotionally from a disappointing snake hunt."

"You know, with your terrific intuition and intelligence, undoubtedly you married well."

Their riotous laughter awakened Humphrey from his morning nap. He jumped and spun around, barking at some unknown mind invasion.

Dan did put the bird-spotting adventure for the grasshopper sparrow together that very day. He was as persuasive with his buddies as a prairie preacher during tornado season. First, he checked with his state friends, downstate, making sure he and his buddies would be welcome. Their answer was a solid invitation to add four pair of eyes to the search for any additional grasshopper sparrow pockets of location, beyond the seven known places where they verifiably had been seen clinging to habitat.

They were good to go!

Dan told everyone that he would spring for the gas, food, and motel bill if they would simply come to help with their game faces on, showing his brand of enthusiasm. Delbert's energy promise was a given and George and Duffy seemed to relish a change of pace idea away from their often monotonous work routine.

Within a week after Delbert and Dan returned from the python hunt, the four of them were on their way south into the sparsely-populated interior of south central Florida. Dan's camouflaged Land Rover, sporting the well-known *Real Florida Outdoors* bear-and-panther logo, was stocked with four talkative friends, and laden down with coolers rattling with water bottles expecting a later infusion of ice, four pair of powerful binoculars, four strong camp stools, four stout walking sticks, and four duffel bags chocked full with clean, old clothes.

A collection of floppy hats and sweat-stained ball caps lay strewn across the dashboard and across seats and a fifth duffel bag filled with an assortment of energy bars, energy drinks, sunblock containers, and various first-aid items took up temporary residency on the floor between the big, booted feet of Duffy.

Dan also had a snakebite kit hidden deep in the glove compartment, its safe presence not advertised on purpose. Secreted as well was his licensed Sturm and Ruger revolver in a zipped case with ammo, protection against unforeseen trouble, that he always stored snugly under his driverside seat. Everyone had their own cell phone. Dan carried some ultra-fancy technology gadgets on his handheld mega-invention that could find Santa Claus asleep in the Amazon Rain Forest.

Two, now empty coolers would carry all manner of food for the three-day vigil, chow they would buy at grocery stores and familiar fast food icons before they virtually left civilization to enter the backcountry domain of the fading grasshopper sparrow. Completing their collected gear for their adventure was a strong telescope with tripod, two digital cameras, and Dan had also brought four spiral notebooks and reliable pens so any and all could make pertinent notations while they were on high alert trying to spot the elusive grasshopper sparrow.

They would do some hiking off-road, some mildly difficult wandering came with the territory, but they didn't plan really long hikes, advancing age for all looming as a deterrent there.

Patience and persistence would be key to any success they might happily report. Long hours of quietude with their vigil melding into part of the landscape would orchestrate their earnest approach.

Dan's plan, concocted in his furtive mind that first night, the whole idea neoned through his brain, was shared with the state wildlife authorities by phone before their trip. It received rave agreement, and was saluted as a great idea. Knowing that the little grasshopper sparrow had been spotted at seven established habitat sites all within thirty miles of each other, a fact that carried a great deal of verifiable evidence, Dan reasoned that it would be helpful, super helpful, with more actual time to save extinction if action were swift and dedicated, to try to expand solid evidence of further range to increase the chances of dealing with even more birds than the ornithologists had estimated. If they could establish broader habitat, even a small amount, it would buy precious time for the good of saving the species from a dismal benediction.

Dan explained his plan in the Land Rover headed toward Osceola and Okeechobee counties and a late breakfast meeting with state biologist Scott Miles outside Okeechobee City. Everyone liked his idea. They ratified his thinking heartily.

Concluding his comments, opening his hands on the steering wheel, Dan said, "Senseless to reinvent the wheel, searching for the little guy where

169

indisputable evidence reveals his declining presence. We would, in essence, be replowing already plowed ground."

"Yes! Yes! Right on! Agreed!" was their Land Rover chorus.

"Maybe, just maybe, by looking between these seven known spots and then casting a larger net of observation around the periphery of known habitat, we can discover some new habitat, theirs all along, but unknown to we humans trying to judge the proven extent of viable living."

"That woulda be neat-o," fisted Delbert.

"Absolutely," quickly replied Dan.

"Great if it happens," nodded Duffy.

"The little guy would be in the news, if found anywhere adjacent to known habitat, and it would focus even more reason to initiate captive-breeding and thereby nurse the grasshopper sparrow back to a sustainable population."

Dan sailed on, a sermon with passion.

"We're not looking for any print for ourselves, any cheers for us. No way. Let's just see if perhaps we can get real lucky and identify some old habitat as still existing habitat. We might just get the public behind the survival from extinction by revealing something new that will get legs in print and on the boob tube with the media folks."

"Yes. Now you're talking," urged George.

"Who knows, even a blind hog finds an acorn now and again. We might get lucky. Three days probably won't do it, but if we get one iota of evidence, we'll be back like Arnold in the movies. Right guys?"

"Will do! Sounds like a deal to me! Count me in."

"Just give us a decent reason, just a whiff of new evidence, and we'll come back. Often."

Dan was proud of his forceful natural world thumping. But, he couldn't snatch the entire credit, he admitted privately. He knew that the beautiful open countryside they were passing, a far cry from the congestion of home turf up Orlando way, released a secret appreciation for countryside, a basic, underlying need for wilderness, singing in the hearts of his passengers, even without their knowledge. Delbert was the exception, of course, his appreciation was open, obvious and vocal.

Scott Miles was already seated in the mom-and-pop diner just north of Okeechobee City, when the Victory Wagon from just northeast of greater Orlando pulled up in soft sand and parked.

Scott Miles, seeing them approach through a glass window, rose to greet them, telling, with eye contact, smile, and handshake to each, how much he appreciated their volunteer time to help in the effort to save the grasshopper sparrow. Breakfast was a hearty meal, after the two-hour drive, and conversation was spirited, fanned along by the very recent memory of Dan's urging rant they all had absorbed driving down to the last, clinging refuge of the grasshopper sparrow.

Scott had a surprise for everyone, and when he produced it from a file in his briefcase, Dan let out a war whoop. His biologist friend had computer-created color pictures of the grasshopper sparrow, a little larger than life size, which he passed around to everyone.

"A help with identification," said Scott. "Like the police and crime folks. Here's a mug shot of the little guy that might help you, if your three-day vigil turns up, hopefully, some new evidence of some old habitat still in use beyond the seven charted pockets of shrinking habitat."

"Would you believe," fairly shouted Dan, "I have similar pictures in my duffel bag, color prints like yours, Scott. I was going to pass mine around too, just before all of us spread out to start our vigil in prairie grasslands of your suggestion. Unreal!"

"You know what they say, 'great minds think alike'," quipped Scott.

"Yours and who else," smirked Dan, with a dig about himself.

Scott gave a map to Dan, an overview of the entire known remaining range of the grasshopper sparrow, with neat notations sketched across it, showing the seven proven habitat locations, different places he suggested they might stakeout near the known habitat, and side information in the margins, detailing dirt roads leading nowhere really, they might follow off main secondary hardtop to ease their vehicular path to prime vigil spots.

Dan paid for breakfast, and they said their goodbyes, wishing each other the best, with a kind of locker room pep talk that wildfired to everyone. Scott and Dan promised to converse several times daily during their three-day vigil on behalf of a dear, little critter weighing about an ounce.

They scoped out a non-frill motel and checked in, two single beds in two rooms, window air-conditioners, creaking linoleum flooring, definitely a hunter refuge in season that wasn't on any touristy chamber of commerce list. It suited them fine. They would all be so tired each day, propped up on those uncomfortable camp stools all day long in the advancing hot May sun, they would flop into bed, not caring where they slept.

They iced down their coolers, and quickly sorted and stacked their gear at the Hi-Lo Motel, bumping into each other with eager anticipation, anxious to hit the prairie grasslands to begin facing the unknown, their well-intentioned vigil with the outcome, a huge question mark looming real.

By one o'clock, with seven hours of daylight remaining in the day, Dan had driven nineteen miles northwest from their breakfast powwow with Scott Miles, stopping well down a bumpy, washboard path, liberally called a road, a place so secluded the vista looked as though it belonged on a different planet.

The view was breathtaking, tree hammocks on the horizon, wave after wave of bunch grasses, bluestem and wiregrass, and a sprinkling of saw palmetto and low shrubs as far as the eye could see across the seemingly endless savannah. Not one house, nor any human-made structure of any kind blighted the surreal landscape.

Dan dropped Duffy first, pointing out a clump of palmetto he thought would be a good home base for his vigil. Duffy studied his hundred-yard hike, laden down with iced cooler, camp stool, hiking stick, binoculars, and notebook. He was so excited he almost forgot to plop his Tampa Bay Rays ball cap atop his balding head. Dan noticed that he had the morning newspaper sports section from home folded and exposed from a shirt pocket. He lifted it out deftly as Duffy began to walk. Duffy felt practically naked without the sports page.

"Ole friend, as project leader, I have to pull rank. Now you know as well as I know, with your sports section you won't be looking for our grasshopper sparrow friend as much as we all should be, plus, plus, you'll fall asleep on that camp stool and then you'll fall off and break a couple of bones."

"Yeah, you're right," grumbled Duffy. "I wasn't thinking."

"No problem, thanks for not getting mad."

Off went Duffy, smiling.

Delbert was dropped next. Dan wanted his backcountry expert between Duffy and George, in case of any emergency. They were being placed about

173

three hundred yards apart, visible to each other, and within the range of a yelling shout.

George went next, walking to a mutually selected location and then Dan pulled the Land Rover over to a grassy road shoulder farther down the road, and selected his own location. The four of them were strung out over a half-mile of distance. In their pockets, they all carried two pictures of their precious quarry, color pictures of the grasshopper sparrow created by Scott Miles and Dan. The enlarged computer pictures were similar but not exactly alike.

Earlier, after breakfast, while Dan was driving to their first chance site, Dan had everyone study the pictures. He gave a running commentary on all the identification markings he could possibly emphasize. If a grasshopper sparrow chanced by their vigil, there was an excellent chance that anyone in this neophyte collection of shadetree ornithologists could identify the tiny bird correctly.

Everyone settled down to their surveillance duties, feeling the strange sensation of utter stillness steal over them. Initially, it was a feeling of eerie misplacement for Duffy and even George. However, as the afternoon dozed along, and they began to detect faint, natural sounds coming from the living savannah itself, they relaxed and reveled in the solitude, as Delbert and Dan, wilderness pros, had done from their very first moments at their posts.

The four became excellent stewards of their volunteering. Duffy and George especially loved the quiet change of pace from their hectic lives. Notebooks were filling with comments for later study and evaluation. However, no grasshopper sparrows flew by to say "Howdy."

Not wanting to wear out his troops at first day battle, Dan gathered them up, one after another, at five in the late afternoon and started the dusty drive back to their fleabag motel. He was surprised at the lively conversation bounding around the Land Rover as they left field study. He had reasoned that they would be quiet, somewhat afflicted with some burnout from May warmth, uncomfortable camp stools, and no positive results. Seeing and listening to their good-natured banter, pulled him immediately into the happy conversation, as he bumped along toward civilization. Dan stuck to the central theme of their presence with his normal upbeat exuberance.

"Tomorrow is another day. Two sites tomorrow morning and afternoon, so we can have a cool break at noon, refreshed with air-conditioning moving from the first site to the second. That will break the day up a little."

"Good idea," agreed Duffy.

"Hey, that sounds great. Good move," added George.

"Mebbe wein be one of dem blind hogs tomorra, and find unsins some lil' sparrow fellas 'stead of dem acorns," exclaimed Delbert.

"That's the spirit," championed Dan.

Some excellent barbeque and hot showers at the Hi-Lo had them happily content and sleepy by 8:30 p.m. They all hit the proverbial hay before 9:00 p.m. Shucks, neither room had a television, only clattering window air-conditioners. And, the stack of magazines that they asked permission to borrow from the motel office were seven years old. It was only a question of who could fall asleep first, so snoring wouldn't keep the other roommate awake.

Refreshed by a decent night's sleep, only interrupted by yowling cats outside and the loud, labored drone of window air-conditioners inside, the four troubadours on a mission rolled out of their sagging mattresses and quickly dressed for a new day in the field with expectations running high.

After stomach fortification with cheese grits, biscuits and white gravy, and link sausage, the now "old pros" to the art of bird watching climbed aboard the Land Rover with shared vocal excitement. When the coolers received a fresh addition of cubed ice and everyone had double-and-triple checked their gear for the day, Dan headed out of Burgsville in nearly the same direction as day one.

However, he exited onto another teeth-rattling dirt road near the one selected, with a mutual groan heard from the previous day. The Land Rover billowed clouds of dusty clay that they all swore could be seen from the international space station. Their destination this second day was twenty-one miles, not just nineteen.

As he drove, clenching the steering wheel, Dan explained his plan.

"We are going to try our luck still outside the seven-site pocket area authorities had confirmed. But, this afternoon, we will invade that blanketed seven-site area to see what we turn up inside. We won't be anywhere near those seven pinpointed locations, no closer than four miles. So, if we spot grasshopper sparrows this afternoon, there won't be any confusion. That good fortune would be a new habitat site, newly confirmed."

Everyone nodded agreement. What could they say? No one had enough grasshopper sparrow knowledge to challenge his ideas, nor would they challenge Dan on any general principles whatsoever.

Dan continued explaining the battle plan and broadened his discussion of their elusive quarry.

"These little guys are very sedentary, usually occupying the same four to five acre territory during their entire life span of two to three years. They often appear feeble in flight, often seeming more willing to run along the ground. So, yesterday was a breeze

176

sitting on our cans on those killer camp stools. Today, roam around, venture around a little. Not long distances, but expand your field of vision and include ground study as you go. And, please, I don't want to worry you, but, please, no, repeat, no snake bites. This is rattlesnake country, big time. When you leave your coolers and camp stools, your hiking sticks go with you. Always. Like you're a Siamese twin attached to those hiking sticks, your defense in thick grass against snakes. And don't be afraid to make a little noise as you go. If you scare up a little guy to flight, all the better, and identification might be easier. Again, we're all married to that hiking stick when we venture out, on say fifteen minute or so short hikes away from our command posts. Got me?"

Everyone nodded vigorously, almost expecting punishment for violation of Dan's directives, as if they were raw recruits in the company of a seasoned battle commander.

Dan dropped everyone off in the same order as the previous day, taking the last lookout position himself. The landscape was similar to their first day vigil, solitary sabal palms, clumps of hardy saw palmetto, and endless stretches of wiregrass.

The morning crept along. It was not as warm as the previous day. It was still early May, and puny Florida-style cold fronts with temperature highs at upper seventies often occurred as delicious lingering spring resisted summer soon to invade. Dan heard no shouts along the picket line of intent observers. He drifted slightly melancholic, knowing full well that silence obviously meant no sightings. He wanted so badly for their hours in the field to turn positive and produce decisive results. He put his game face back on though when he picked everyone up for lunch. He couldn't appear sullen or detached, his role was cheerleader despite the score and he played the part.

Lunch, sitting in a circle on a clear spot of earth, under a copse of turkey oaks near a one-acre pond, munching store-bought sandwiches and snacks, was jovial, with Dan leading a comedy hour of jokes and light banter, attempts to divert thoughts from the long afternoon ahead. His sitdown schtick was crowd pleasing, everyone remained focused.

Delbert livened things up by sharing that he had heard and then glimpsed a rattlesnake beyond his measured step in the long grass on one of his exploring hikes, but the potential bad boy had moved on as he poked his way along with his trusty hiking stick as shield.

Without the crutch of air-conditioning, not needed on the spring day that also boasted a cool breeze, Dan drove his squad to a new location for the afternoon vigil. This one, as explained to his troops earlier, was inside the perimeter of the seven sites known and identified, but it was new grasshopper sparrow grassland to inspect.

Again, he dropped everyone off in the same order, but bunched everyone together by a hundred yards or so, enhancing shouting distance in a form of unspoken luck he didn't share. The indomitable four settled down to campstool radar duty, vision style, and short reconnaissance soirees in different directions from their iced-cooler headquarters. They were growing accustomed to their routine, as if they had done it all before in some previous life.

The comfortable warmest part of the day passed. Sighing and slumping alone with his thoughts, Dan glanced at his watch, noting 3:38 p.m., when he detected a faint shout from George down the picket line.

"Delbert! Delbert! Delbert! Found! Found!" were the cryptic words, as best he could distinguish.

Dan walk-jogged back to George, who met him about halfway from his own post. George repeated his message, blurting it out, stumbling over his words.

Red-faced, he spilled golden words.

"Delbert ran down, part way to me, just a couple of minutes ago. He kept shouting, coming near. 'Found three. Found three,' he kept saying. He said 'On the ground, then flying low'."

"Whoopee! No fooling! Gigantic news. Delbert got a sighting. It had to be Delbert."

"Yup," roared George.

"I'll run back and get the Land Rover. Pick you up on the way back, and we'll get to that rascal Delbert."

Dan jogged to his metal steed, leaving his gear in the field, and sped back to George waiting in the middle of the dirt road. They saw Delbert within moments, waving his arms over his head in a victory salute. The three men, led by Delbert, retraced the path of one of his short hikes and Dan and George were shown the exact spot where he had spotted three grasshopper sparrows.

"Ain't no mistake. Me a-lookin' at dem pictures a million time since Mr. Scott and you give dem to usins. And, I knowt sparrows anyhow. It was him. Three lil' birds. Marked up da same. Weak a-flyin'. All of dem things we been a-studyin'. Ain't no question."

"I believe you. I believe you," assured Dan, slapping Delbert on his back. Had the sighting been reported by Duffy or George he would have had some doubt. But, with the sighting reported by Delbert, he had no doubt about its accuracy.

Momentarily, overcome with the weight of decision-making and the euphoria accompanying the sighting, Dan double-clutched on what to do next.

179

But, in a very few seconds, his immediate future was crystal clear.

Four hours of daylight remained. He needed desperately to get cell phone reception to Scott Miles in the hope he could get him and his fellow biologists out to Delbert's sighting site that very day so a true confirmation could be won.

Leaving their gear where it all lay in the field with excitement reigning the moment, Dan beeped down the road for Duffy and soon he emerged in the distance lugging his cooler, campstool, and hiking stick. Duffy was immediately told the details of Delbert's sighting and joined the praise party.

Dan lurched down the road as fast as the surface roughness would allow. Everyone steadied their hats on their heads. Repeatedly, Dan tried to get a good signal to reach Scott Miles and finally, after eight miles, he scored with a connection. His excitement was a neon billboard.

"Could you come now, Scott?" pled Dan. "It would mean a great deal to us if you could. None of us will sleep a wink tonight until we get confirmation or bad news, if it has to be that. I believe Delbert's evidence without question. He's simply that good with all things in the natural world. Can you come?"

Dan gasped for air, and waited for Scott's answer.

"You will! Great! Three hours plus of daylight! You're a gem, Scott. Yes. Yes. Close to an old, rundown cattle dipping pen, with the shoot still intact. You know the road and the cattle pen, right? We'll meet you along that road by that disbanded cattle pen and we'll lead you in. Our gear is still in the field. We alerted you as soon as we could."

Dan shut up and listened to Scott, uttering only a series of the word "yes." Then, he concluded speaking with a wide-eyed look around to everyone.

"Forty-five minutes. Wow! You're practically on the road. Great. Bye. And, thanks a million."

Dan snapped shut his cell phone and fisted the air in triumph. With the Land Rover a beehive of buzzing activity, he wheeled her around and drove the six miles back to the time-imploded cattle dipping pen. They had enough time to retrieve their gear but decided to wait. Green as grass, they were with the excitement, thinking that going back to gather up gear just perhaps might disturb the little sparrows and mess up everything.

So, they parked and waited. An eternity! They all drifted reverently silent. Some prayed. Some hummed and fidgeted. Dan looked in his rearview mirror every twenty-five seconds, looking for clouds of clay dust that would signal Scott's arrival. Wristwatch hands seemed frozen from movement. Time inched along, they sat with windows open, drinking in the hypnotizing sounds of the savannah, a magnificent vista that had the power to be so gracious to them if the sighting could be substantiated with certainty.

Finally, a rising billow of dusty clay behind them signaled the arrival of Scott Miles, who pulled up alongside with another biologist riding shotgun with him. Scott signaled for Dan to lead the way, and he didn't need a second invitation to guide Scott back to Delbert's sighting spot.

All six men stood briefly together in the middle of the washboard road, talking and pointing. Dan's crew had shut their Land Rover doors so quietly, not to disturb the little sweethearts, one would have thought they had arrived at a church for a funeral.

"No guarantees, you realize," solemned Scott. "We may not see a thing, but that result may not rule out anything positive."

"Oh, I know," assured Dan. "No guarantees, of course, but maybe we'll get lucky. Got to think that way."

"Perhaps," doled Scott, without fanfare.

Scott and newly-introduced Glenn carried high-powered binoculars, a two-foot long telescope without the tripod, many cameras, and each clutched a knobby, sturdy hiking stick poised against any rattlesnake wars.

"You guys cool it in the Land Rover. Glenn and I will go in alone and see what we can see. We don't want half the county marching in, do we?"

"No," agreed Dan.

His crew gingerly stepped back into the Land Rover, again closing the doors softly. Scott and Glenn started off into the thigh-high wiregrass.

The Land Rover became a mausoleum of silence, everyone trying to wait patiently for news from Scott and Glenn. All of them, the four devoted explorers, embraced their own private thoughts, and didn't want to spook good news. Avoidance of each other was like a bench of baseball players separating themselves from their pitcher late in a game quest for a no-hitter.

Their agonizing wait was not long, even though it seemed like an entire Ice Age to those quietly imprisoned in the Land Rover. In thirty-five minutes, Scott and Glenn appeared in the distance, and then drew ever closer with deadpan expressions drawn down across their sun-burnished faces. As they arrived, their expressions remained somber. Dan and his buddies sank in spirit, hope snatched away in all their mourning minds.

Scott spoke first to the upstate group reassembled in a slumping huddle outside the Land Rover. He should have won an Academy Award nomination.

"Well," he began, "I can safely say, without any contradiction, that known remaining habitat for grasshopper sparrows now stands at eight, not seven."

Scott burst into a broad smile and raised two cluttered arms in triumph.

Dan and his buddies didn't assemble the mathematics for a few moments. Then, they all did at once when they saw Scott in his victory salute.

Pandemonium in the savannah!

There was as much hugging and high-five tributes all around as Little Leaguers winning at Williamsport.

"Maybe we made a little difference," Dan kept saying. "Maybe just a little difference."

Scott and Glenn assured everyone that they had indeed made a difference and that their discovery of a new habitat site would make the news and draw more positive focus to the plight of the grasshopper sparrow.

Delbert, Dan, Duffy, and George called their wives with the great news when they returned to civilization, their aptly named Burgsville. After another barbeque feast, Dan surprised everyone by stopping at a skimpy grocery store where he bought two six-packs of beer.

At the Hi-Lo Motel, in a dignified adult state, they had a victory party that evening. Three beers apiece, their limit, was no alarm for drunkenness defended Dan.

Well into their first beer at a rare beer outing for all, held in one of their two rooms, Dan made a little speech surrounded by his buddies and an occasional, darting cockroach.

"It will be a victory ride home early in the morning. I'm proud of all of us. Tremendously so. We can't say we saved the grasshopper sparrow. No we can't and won't. However, we may have made a difference, ever so slight, because the important issue

183

of their predicted extinction will get a news boost, not mentioning us by name, but noteworthy news that may help focus renewed effort to change the course of what is happening to the grasshopper sparrow so that we can avoid a repeat of the sad, sad end of the dusky seaside sparrow a few years ago."

Delbert, Duffy, and George raised their beers in a cheer. Delbert's beer was unopened. He never, never drank, but he certainly knew how to get excited over all matters pertaining to the glory of the natural world.

Dan, standing, concluded with a poignant soliloquy.

"Wouldn't it be great sometime in the future, to have *Audubon Magazine* do a news story about our little guy, the grasshopper sparrow, changing their caption from their March/April issue this year when they warned, 'End of the line.' I know they would be delighted to do exactly that. Who knows, guys, maybe we really did make an ever-so-slight difference."

CHAPTER IX

Within two weeks after returning from south-central Florida, where the fantastic success of locating an additional pocket of grasshopper sparrow habitat made news stories all across the sunshine state, cocky summer, with all its wilting fury, rode into Florida towns everywhere, like the bullying arrival of an infamous gunslinger in the days of the Old West.

Summer in Florida redefined seasons. Summer lasted for more than the seasonal three-month dole of time allotted on calendars. Summer demanded and reluctantly received more, a six-month torment holiday, brushing aside with weapons of pelting rain and blistering heat any rebuttal that it came to visit for only three months like the other three, well-behaving seasons. Summer was the nasty rogue for as long as folks could remember.

Six months boasted summer from its lofty bully pulpit. I'll leave when I always do, long about

Halloween, but six months is my stay time. And, the Florida folks fought back with only puny weapons like air conditioning, swimming pools, and squirting hoses, umbrellas, hats, iced liquids, all limpy sticks and stones against brutal summer, the fire-breathing dragon.

If summer could talk, it would laughingly say, "You can run but you can't hide. You still have to go outside, then you are mine."

The Miller family and the Turner family played hide-and-seek with that golden eye in the sky every summer as such was the only flimsy option grabbed by millions of other Floridians. Going places outside early or late if you were fortunate enough to be able to control your life in that manner was the universal plan.

Dan's ecotourism business at *Real Florida Outdoors* declined sharply during the summer months. They still conducted nature lectures inside under air-conditioning, but the ranks of attending guests depleted in summer. Schools were taking their normal long break, so field trips for students were interrupted. Snowbirds went north chasing cooler temperatures and seniors, taken on short, supervised hikes other seasons of the year, huddled inside, avoiding the broil of summer. It was a time of assessment, repair, tweaking of known systems going forward, preparation days directed toward making the *Real Florida Outdoors* experience even better when the true fall-into-spring business season revved up again in late September.

Lily, with strong tenure years in her favor, usually taught only two graduate-level humanities courses at the nearby university during the summer. It was her slow time of year, a period when she stayed current with good books and other cultural tools of her scholastic trade. She did some gardening across the lovely grounds of *Le Terrier de Renard*, venturing out with work gloves and trowel only early in the morning and late, late afternoons near sunset.

Mae Ella and Delbert weathered the rude smack of summer with creative work conducted inside, Mae Ella, at her work station outfitted with a green visor eyeshade and her telescoped magnifying glass attached about her pretty head with a flexible cord. Her array of hot wattage lamps, pliers, cutting tools, and nearly microscopic wire and clasps, looked like paraphernalia appropriate for a dentist or a software repairman.

She divided her craft time between designing decorative jewelry and making distinctive quilts, both talented creations never failing to stir talkative praise among the browsing and buying public at seasonal craft shows. Her quilts always were awarded ribbons at judged shows if not the top prize itself.

Delbert busied himself with his wooden birdhouses, building about a hundred each summer for his hopeful contribution toward family sales at the twenty-two craft shows that they attended as vendors during the cooler months. He had converted a spare bedroom at their modest bungalow in Oak Hill into a neat shop, a suggestion by Mae Ella that he come indoors out of the heat with his advancing age a possible concern.

He still whirred his loud skill saw between twin sawhorses on the open back porch, cutting to his exacting specifications the various pieces of his birdhouse creations, but he carefully transported inside armloads of birdhouse parts, leaving messy sawdust outside, away from cluttering the neat, clean house Mae Ella always kept.

By early August each year, they had constructed enough home crafts, ready for sale, to adorn every jewelry fancier within a nine-county radius and to please every home-seeking bird within the same nine-county area.

Thusly, late August and early September were twiddle-thumbs months for Mae Ella and Delbert with well more merchandise stacked around the house than they would need for the wallet-opening public come craft-season time. Of course, as needed diversion throughout the summer, Delbert would ride along with Dan on various natural world adventures and he would study lecture material that he would present as second banana color during the height of the lecture season at *Real Florida Outdoors*, a time of year, cooler weather, that coincided with their slate of craft shows.

To shoo away late summer monotony, Mae Ella did a lot of baking and she experimented with new recipes, all of which Delbert loved without exception.

And, they both went shelling early mornings and late afternoons along the Atlantic Ocean in Brevard County, filling cardboard boxes to the brim with eye-catching shells of all shapes, colors, and textures. They placed the best ones as Florida heirlooms all around their bungalow once the sun had dried them and their sharp, pungent natural odor had been dispelled in the drying process.

But, this summer was no ordinary summer, not by any means. Not by any normal standard!

This summer was preparation and planning time for a really big and special event, the upcoming October roast-toast for one Delbert Turner, a priceless individual, now up in years, who had touched the lives of hundreds upon hundreds of people with his innocent, modest, and inimitable brand of outdoor skills, garnering, in that process, the heartfelt plaudits of many, even a sitting United States President when he once joined at a Rose Garden White House ceremony eighteen other environmental heroes from other states, who received a handshake, personal applause, private meeting time, and a special plaque from the President himself, as a salute to their passionate care for the living, natural world.

Indeed, no ordinary summer in east-central Florida!

Delbert's admirers organizing the October event were determined to keep it all a surprise for Delbert, right up to his motoring arrival that autumn Saturday. They fully knew that their wish would be some chore to accomplish. They concentrated on secretive steps to help ensure the element of surprise, their first approach being a strict following to the old familiar saying about secrets:

The fewer who know increases the chance of success.

Mae Ella did all her telephone calling at the home of a friend who lived close by and scarcely knew Delbert, going there to work on the project when Delbert was away tromping in the woods or swamps with Dan and his buddies. She made her own cell phone off limits too, although Delbert never searched her phone memory for messages. She didn't use her computer at home, as Delbert bounced to its mystique on occasion, playing with the screens and keyboard like a kid who was playing with a toy too sophisticated for his skill level.

When Delbert planned to be away from their home for many hours, Mae Ella sped over to *Le Terrier de Renard* to use Lily's computer and telephone. Both she and Lily were as busy as proverbial beavers all summer long, seeing the whole event happily organize itself as the months were torn from calendars.

June!

Then July!

Dan opened and paid for a private mailbox in Sanford, with the intent that all snail mail would funnel through it. The inner committee, Mae Ella, Lily and Dan, even had letterhead and envelopes printed, carrying the Sanford post office address without Delbert's name actually appearing in print. There was no evidence trail back to Mae Ella and Delbert's bungalow, neither telephone nor computer, and certainly not idle conversation that became suspicious.

They were in a wartime mode, ultra-careful but without scary blackouts or the rationing of vital goods!

Dan was dynamite with the big stuff, organizing work parties for the transport of table and chairs, invitation contact with county and state bigwigs, finalizing who would present actual toasts, coordination of music and adequate sound systems, reserving a podium and a good microphone, assembling a Powerpoint tribute for Delbert's life, conferences with media friends at newspapers and television stations he could swear to secrecy until event time.

Mae Ella and Lily handled the menu end of things, food and drink, and a zillion incidentals also like a formal sign-in book, flowers for the tables, cut out table markers capturing Delbert's profile with his omnipresent ballcap he wore constantly, janitorial teams to clean the nature center and its bathrooms, making sure the kitchen would be ready and the commercial freezer empty enough ahead of time to store the ice and food dishes they would need for upwards of one hundred and twenty-five guests.

September disappeared from calendars! The countdown started! Clocks ticked loudly, mocking the chance of oversights!

"Napkins," shouted Mae Ella to Lily one day in early October when they were together checking off items completed on their master list of needs.

The Saturday in late October finally arrived, and prayers were answered. The day broke cloudless and remained cloudless and the air carried an actual hint of coolness. Spirits were sky-high!

Dan agreed to act as master of ceremonies, an obvious choice and he promised to keep his comments short as he proceeded to introduce the list of presenters who would speak about their highly memorable times spent with Delbert, experiencing some of his outstanding Florida backcountry magic.

The Delbert Turner Nature Center in the Wahaweechee State Park had been scrubbed until it gleamed and sparkled. Its many exhibits had been dusted and whipped clean with caring, slow-proceeding hands. Its terrariums and aquariums breathed pristine condition. Mae Ella and Lily had a volunteer army of culinary helpers around them, all of whom had been scurrying around since early Saturday morning. Everything deliciously edible was in place and ready to serve.

All systems relative to power sockets were working perfectly. Amplification had been tested and was sounding perfect, no humming vibrations. The tables were festooned with wild flowers, bromeliads, orchids, and neat clumps of Spanish moss. Dan had a dozen employees from his *Real Florida Outdoors* in attendance outside, ready to direct parking, and to assist a police detail in any way asked. The two bands were set and ready to play, and they knew each other well, so no jealousy would interfere with musical artistry played for the enjoyment of the happy throng.

The event team was ready. The second-guessing was over.

Lily said emphatically to Dan, her lovely hair already drooping across her forehead, "Even if we mess up now somewhere, even more than once, we have enough going for us as it stands right now, to make this a huge success."

"Exactly," agreed Dan. "No worries. I sense a great success, and special salutes go to you and Mae Ella."

"Thank you, honey. We worked hard."

"Truly you did. In capable loving hands. You and Mae Ella."

Folks started to arrive well before eleven o'clock. The beautiful, cool day, one of the first of the season, gave everyone the energy boost to feel very good about going somewhere important. Signing the guest book was a prideful act of appreciation. Folks adored Delbert. And, they loved the bluegrass and country music filling the nature center, as they browsed around exhibits and then later happily found their own name card placed at their designated table.

Duffy and George had drawn the special spy assignment of picking up Delbert in Oak Hill, a welcomed chore they viewed as an honor. The event committee had debated what ruse to use to continue the secrecy and yet get Delbert with them, looking hopefully cleanly dressed and yet natural and comfortable for the popping and silent cameras. They decided upon a convincing lie. They sprung on Delbert two days before the event the concocted story that they all had to meet at the nature center to answer media questions and have their pictures taken, relative to their grasshopper sparrow success five months earlier.

Delbert bought the story and even sat quietly without fidgeting when Mae Ella gave him a haircut and he agreed to wear the clean, pressed clothes Mae Ella carefully laid out for him. She even washed his favorite ballcap twice through the washer, but evidence of most of his sweat stains remained.

So far, so good on total secrecy, they all cheerfully reasoned!

Dan drifted around the nature center enjoying the music as guests arrived, mixing freely with dignitaries from Tallahassee, city and county commissioners, several prominent members of Florida Fish and Wildlife, and just plain folks he had known for years. The governor and members of his cabinet were not present, but they had sent long letters of congratulation that Dan would read later to the happy throng. He made a point of telling each roast-and-toast presenter when they would be on the program, using a little prompt card he carried in a shirt pocket. He had a backup duplicate tucked away in a rear pants pocket.

When they arrived, Duffy and George flanked Delbert as they walked toward the festivities, hopeful he wouldn't fall down faint from all the commotion. Instead, he remarked with an innocent one-liner that made them both howl.

"Dat dare lil' grasshopper sparrow, one ounce little, done cause a heap big crowd."

They were well inside, in the seating and band area before Delbert finally tumbled with the realization that the whole reason for the gathering was him. Balloons, posters with his name blazoned, and applause, with people turning toward him as they clapped, were quite obvious clues. It wasn't that Delbert was slow or stupid, only unassuming and modest, two of his very best and abiding qualities. Mae Ella and Lily rushed to him and kissed him. Mae Ella was crying with joy and pride.

"Surprised?" beamed Mae Ella, hugging him.

"Rekon I is! Plum surprised. What all the big fuss about?"

"Y-O-U! a salute to your life past, silly! But you still have a long time to live! Promise!"

"Well, I'll be," managed Delbert, shaking his head in deep ponder mode.

When everyone had arrived, one hundred and twenty-four strong, a dozen or so more than expected, Dan, at the microphone, coaxed everyone to their seats. Privately, he thanked himself for having extra tables and chairs at the ready. A pledge of allegiance to the American flag and a prayer by a Methodist minister officially launched their party.

Dan returned to the microphone, and released everyone to a quickly forming buffet line.

"We are serving both sides of the buffet table, identical hunger-stoppers on both sides, favorite dishes just for you, created by some of Delbert's expert cooking friends. So, the line should move right along."

The two bands, taking turns, in their corner of the large hall, where some exhibits had to be moved to accommodate tables and chairs, played stomach-friendly music throughout lunch, leaving the John Philip Sousa rousing and stirring stuff for the introduction of the parade of speakers later. The band members had sampled plates of food earlier in the nature center kitchen. They weren't hungry.

There was a warm buzz of conversation and laughter as folks dove into the dazzling array of special down-home recipes begging to be claimed. Of course, radiant Mae Ella and Delbert, still a little baffled by all the attention, sat at the head table along with Lily and

Dan, Edna and Duffy, Clara and George, and the minister. The Tallahassee bigwigs apologizing profusely that the governor could not attend as they displayed his hand-written note of good wishes, sat together, friendly enough they were, but they clung together, despite Dan's best urgings that they mix with total strangers. Things weren't as rigid at other tables, where mingling of different folks sat together, strangers to each other, blending with knots of friends.

A dozen women, including Mae Ella and Lily served dessert, direct to the tables, trays with generous slices of key lime pie topped with scoops of vanilla ice cream. The delivery alone before anyone munched a bite drew applause. The State of Florida designated pie in huge abundance. What a treat!

While folks finished up lunch with dessert, nodding vigorous approval as they slid key lime pie a' la mode down contented throats, Dan clunked his fork against his water glass and addressed the seated throng again.

"We're about to start. Anyone wanting coffee, tea or a fresh drink, kindly get it now. We need to get started. We have a fairly long but very interesting program!"

A few folks scurried to the beverage counter, following Dan's lead. The bands picked up the guitar and banjo tempo a little, and the crowd, nearly silent while engrossed with a delectable lunch, again began to buzz and chatter.

Within short minutes, Dan was again at the microphone. "Thank you all for being here today to honor our dear friend, Delbert Turner. And thank you also everyone for keeping this event secret for so long. That was not easy. Delbert here was totally surprised today, in fact, I think he is still surprised."

Laughter!

195

"I have the distinct feeling that our proceedings today will be more toasts than roasts, don't you?"

"Yes," was the upbeat chorus. A few whistles and even shouts ratified Dan's statement.

Dan scratched his chin, looking pensive, saying, "What in the world could be said against him in the form of a roast? Nothing!"

More laughter.

"Seriously."

Applause and laughter again!

"Some famous person, I forget just who at the moment, once said that when giving a speech or a sermon, the best thing you can do is to have the beginning be as close to the end as possible."

The crowd giggled at Dan's humor.

"So, that being excellent advice, I'll try to abide by that wisdom today and let our parade of toasts relate great experiences with Delbert. With that promise, our first presenter is local, retired cub scout master, Wes Reed."

All the presenters were sitting at tables. Wes threaded his way up to the microphone. "A true honor to be here today," began Wes. "I have the very best memories of Delbert. I was a cub scout master in central Florida for many years, I met Delbert in the Wahaweechee here many years ago, taking scouts out on hikes to help them earn credits toward merit badges. I first met him by the river. He had some live critters – he calls them 'critters' -- in his canoe, a box turtle, a harmless snake in a jar, a small orphaned raccoon. The cubs loved him talking about nature. Then, afterward, as I got to know him better, I started telling him exact dates and times we would be on certain trails out here and he would meet us there always. Soon, each time, he'd be in a huddle with scouts gathered around him, explaining saw palmetto, showing Spanish moss or a bromeliad, two different turtles, one in each hand. Delbert was a true scoutmaster's gift for years and years, describing native Florida in his own great way, making my job easier and the scouts' knowledge better. The fondest memories I have of Delbert, on a trail or by the river. Years and years!"

Wes Reed half turned to Delbert, sitting at the head table, and snapped a military salute in his direction before he exited the podium.

"Joyce Adams, folks. Joyce Adams," greeted Dan.

"Thank you. I must confess that I'm a little embarrassed up here on such an occasion honoring Delbert, because when I first heard about him, I called him 'the wild man of the woods.' How wrong and inconsiderate of me. I should be ashamed and am ashamed. And, I apologize to him and all of you today. All Delbert ever did for me was quite possibly save the life of my son, Todd, and the life of my nephew, Mark. On a cub scout campout here in the Wahaweechee, years ago, Todd and Mark, wandering off where they shouldn't have gone, got lost at night. Helicopters, with searchlights, police and rescue folks couldn't find them, but Delbert did. Looking for them on his own, with his wilderness skills, Delbert found two very tired and frightened boys that night in Alligator Slough. Ever, ever, ever indebted to Delbert. Forever. I am humbled to be here today. And, my sincerest apologies to you, dear Delbert!"

When Joyce Adams left the podium, she blew kisses in Delbert's direction and bowed toward him with a curtsey.

Some folks stood at their tables, joining everyone with applause, as Joyce Adams, now in late middle-age but still an eye-catching beauty, returned to her seat.

Again at the microphone, Dan smiled across to Joyce Adams and bowed in her direction before calling the next presenter.

"Folks, a warm welcome for Esther Taylor."

Esther, aged eighty-seven, was escorted slowly to the podium by her two sons, Slim and Johnny. They stood on either side of her after she waddled to the microphone and began to speak in a gravelly voice.

"Happy day today for the Taylor family, being here to honor Delbert. You see, we folks, our clan, introduced Mae Ella to Delbert. We feel we are partly responsible for their happiness today. Have known Delbert for years. We all used to cut palm fronds out near here for Palm Sunday services at churches in Brevard County and for Seminole Indian crafts down at their reservations. The State of Florida let us. We weren't trespassing. Nothing like that. Delbert would join me, Slim and Johnny here, and a fellow named Old Mule, who passed away last year, and he would help cut and gather green palm fronds. Not killing any trees. All for God and them poor Seminoles the army hunted back well over, well over, a hundred years ago. Delbert and me and my boys used to talk about our panther sightings and such. All of us liked Delbert. Who couldn't like him? He was the best worker and best kind of person you ever did see. And that's why I got our very good family friend, Mae Ella, and him together. And, as you can see here today, they be sweethearts to this glorious day. Praise God!"

Esther waved to Mae Ella and Delbert, before being guided back to her table by her sons. The bluegrass band strummed guitars and banjos in a down home rendition of "The Wedding March."

"Thank you, Esther. Aren't we all glad Mae Ella and Delbert found each other? What say, folks?"

Applause, whistles, and polite shouts.

"Our next presenter is from out of town, so to speak. Norm Palmer, from up past Gainesville a little bit. He has a story to tell you that I know about as it was my privilege to be a part of it in a small way."

"*Let me add my thanks to those already stated up here,*" began Norm. "*How well do we all, north of here about a hundred and thirty miles, appreciate your friend and neighbor down here, Delbert. One of a kind, if there ever was one! He came into our lives for a few, short weeks several years ago. At that time, in the cold of winter, and it can get plenty cold some winters up in cave and cavern country, a long drought we were all suffering through kept a strangle hold on us. Thought it would never, never end. Remember?*

'Sure do," and "yes" were the collective answers from the audience.

"*Well,*" continued Norm, "*some of our lakes got so low, they dried up! And, wouldn't you believe it, becoming exposed in the damp lake bottoms, spread over three lakes in particular, were quite a number of dugout canoe relics that dated back hundreds of years, some thousands of year. Well, the media got hold of the story and blabbed it all over creation and we antiquity folks had one devil of a time holding down the thievery where the ancient canoes sat, while we folks were trying to catalog, date, and preserve them as best as we could and as fast as we could. Well, Delbert here was one of many volunteers who came to our rescue, through Dan here, and his presence proved to be the best thing that ever happened to us. Canoe thieves were slipping in at night, stealing canoes in pickup trucks, coming in with their lights off. Now, it was cold, mind you. Cold! Coordinating with police cruising this big three-lake area, they couldn't rope it all off for protection, here was Delbert, out every night with a five-cell flashlight and a walkie-talkie we gave*

199

him, riding a bicycle we had also in the bitter cold, freeze or near freeze every night, keeping thieves away with blinking flashlight or tipping off the authorities on the main roads if some thief snuck in where he wasn't and then he heard them leave with their lights off. The other volunteers were asleep in warm cabins or the warm temporary tents we erected, heaters in both. Delbert's actions led to arrest and recoveries, and to would-be thieves getting scared and hauling buggy out of Delbert's stakeout range as soon as possible. Later, we learned that the commercial use of the ancient canoes was conversational pieces for fish and hunt camps, decorating around camp fires as foot rests with flowers planted where archaic people once sat with paddles. Delbert saved the day with his nightly vigils, and today these canoes, thoroughly studied and preserved, are all in museums where they should be. Delbert was the difference."

Norm left the microphone, shaking a victory balled fist over his head. Applause chased him back to his table.

"Kind folks, welcome Bruce Lowery from our beloved Florida State Park system. He has a great human interest story to relate about Delbert. And, by the way, in the recent past, Florida, on more than one yearly occasion, has been recognized as the best state park system in the nation."

"Let me also extend my thanks to all for allowing me to tell, here today, this true story about Delbert."

Applause! Folks were having a grand time. Delbert couldn't find a place to hide!

"Several years ago now, Delbert was out one winter day exploring throughout one of our state parks not too far from here, trying to assess the wild hog population, helping we guys stuck too much in office

routine. He wasn't too far from the entrance parking corral, it happened to be, a cold winter day, middle of the afternoon, when one of those small passenger vans from a retirement center pulled in and parked. Field trip! He saw all this from behind clumps of saw palmetto where he was looking for hog evidence. Secretly, he saw about a dozen or so senior citizens get out of the van laden down with binoculars and water bottles. Going bird watching! Delbert thought they had a guide, doubling as the driver. They started to form in a group and then began to leave the parking corral for a rutted path that could quite possibly lead to harm's way in Delbert's thinking. Now, Delbert can be shy. Right? Not a fault, mind you, just a characteristic. Right! Anyhow, his mind snapped to attention! Earlier that day, he had spotted a subsidence hole hidden by weeds just at the side of the path where this group would be walking in a few minutes, looking up for birds, and quite possibly not, repeat, not down at their feet. Now, this subsistence hole, was not a sink hole. It was about four feet deep, and near the top, but hidden. It was the broken edge of a drain pipe that went under the road. Some truck probably broke the edge of the pipe after it was laid and probably the soil bank wasn't packed hard enough to last when the pipe went in. Anyhow, it was a perfect snare to grab an unsuspecting leg. Delbert had noticed it earlier in the day and was definitely going to report it to us through Dan later in the day or the next day. Soon, for sure. So! So! So! Being shy and looking disheveled and dirty from field work, which just happens, Delbert made a split-second decision. He didn't want to frighten them with a warning, and he was afraid that would happen because that had happened before, startling folks, him appearing out of nowhere. So . . . so, still unseen, with just enough time to sneak down the road without being seen, as it

201

twisted and turned a little, and this group of senior citizens were to reach the danger spot in a very few minutes, this leg-breaking cavern, Delbert races quietly, like an old Indian scout in soft moccasins, back down the road, path really, picking up a dead palm frond on the way. Now, it's cold, mind you. Dead of winter. That's when the birds come. Right! Great bird watching. Okay! Anyhow, he gets to the problem area, whips off one of his heavy shirts. He liked to layer heavy shirts in winter, rather than wearing a jacket, he once told me, because without a jacket, he had more arm freedom to work. Anyhow, he peels off his outer shirt, wraps it tightly around the palm frond, and jams his makeshift warning flag down the accident-waiting-to-happen hole, as a signal to the unclued senior citizen group about to draw near, and then trots off in a slow run the two miles to his stashed canoe, off to rendezvous with Dan as soon as possible to get word to us about a lawsuit waiting to happen. Never seen by human eyes. We never heard from any of the bird watchers and Delbert had not seen any identification on the van because it was obscured from view in the parking corral. You can be certain that their guide leader or many in that bird watching procession saw the shirt signal and approached the hole very gingerly and carefully. Quick thinking under pressure. Action and success. That's our Delbert."

A person at a rear table couldn't contain himself, shouting out, "Delbert did you ever get the shirt back?"

Bruce Lowery deferred, turning to Delbert, and asking quietly, "*Delbert?*"

Delbert, red-faced and uncomfortable, with Mae Ella's hand on his shoulder, replied, "It turn up at dat old deer-check-in station 'bout a week later."

The band played feverishly as Bruce Lowery returned to his table. The crowd hooted approval, nicely warming to the festive, special occasion.

"Please welcome from the far northland, but loving Florida now, Henry Sullivan, from Winter Park, who has made his wonderful, wonderful generosity felt all across Central Florida in recent years."

"Old guys, like me, should be brief when we talk before groups, so you can still see us standing at the microphone, rather than hiding unconscious on the floor."

The audience, loving his candor, laughed with him.

"I'm a comparative newcomer to Florida, only here a few years. From Michigan. Love home, but now love Florida just as much. Recovering here from a severe illness while in my seventies, ages ago, I met Mae Ella and Delbert out in our, you note I said 'our' great outdoors. I took to them both immediately, Delbert, the son I never had. I was fortunate enough to have several daughters. My doctors had advised limited time spent in our marvelous state parks, and Delbert agreed to tutor me on all the interesting plants and animals we have here in Florida. From those early acquaintance days, I spent many hours with Mae Ella and Delbert in the cathedral of the great outdoors we have here. I learned so very much and grew to appreciate so very much. The times spent with them were magical moments. They relaxed and healed me. I was even fortunate enough to travel on the St. Johns River with the Millers sitting up here as well as with Mae Ella and Delbert at the same time. No one, believe me, no one had to tell me about his true worth. I already knew. But, I'm having a great time today listening to these presenters talk about him. That last true tale about the shirt, the palm frond, and that hole

203

speaks volumes, doesn't it? Truly great. Thank you for allowing me to speak."

Audible agreement with Henry Sullivan's statement could be heard at table after table across the entire room.

Dan returned to the microphone.

"Everybody doing fine? We have a few more presenters. Stayed tuned up here. Don't you think it safe for me to say now that our event here today is a Delbert toast, not a Delbert roast?"

Applause. Agreement was emphatic.

"Our next presenter is Vern Caldwell from Florida Fish and Wildlife. You'll love his experience with Delbert."

"My thanks are added to those already expressed here today. An honor to be asked to be a part of this wonderful event. Yes, I have a story that took place many years ago, right here in the Wahaweechee. We were having a rash of fish seining in the river inside the park. Unlawful. One pickup truck in particular we would see on occasion parked up in brush outside the park. We suspected the occupants as culprits. We didn't call the police fellows, we tried a business card first, under the truck windshield wiper. Nothing! We didn't see that gray pickup for a time and then saw it again parked at a different spot. We tipped off Delbert to our suspicions, and some hikers had seen two men with a seine down by a stretch of the river. Well, Delbert started keeping an eye out, and would you believe it, about two days later, many of you know Delbert had several canoes and rowboats hidden all along the Wahaweechee, two days later from a hidden perch in forest cover, Delbert watches these two guys throwing this big seine net into the river and having some illicit luck. Delbert told me

later that when they threw it, lead weights at the edges and all, it looked like pizza dough circling in the air, like in one of those pizza commercials. Anyhow, he watches in hiding, never seen, for about an hour. Then, the two guys stop fishing, eat a big lunch, fold up the seine real tidy like, and then wobble back about seventy-five feet or so with bloated stomachs, to take a nap on a small patch of grass up from the sandy shore of the river. They leave their cooler, fish bucket and seine down where they were breaking the law. Delbert edges closer, and when the two of them are snoring like drunks, he slips out of the forest and takes him one big seine under his arm for a one-way trip to Possum Slough."

Laughter everywhere.

"No, it gets better. Delbert has a little devil in him sometimes, so this day it surfaced as it did once in a while. Delbert stayed within earshot of the two sleeping men, hidden in the forest, far enough away to make a safe escape, but close enough to hear any hollering reaction. Well, Delbert told me he waited about fifteen minutes, and then heard an awful ruckus. He said they were using every word in the Sailors Swearing Manual. He lit out, taking secret side trails throughout the Wahaweechee only he knew, chuckling as he loped away. We, at Fish and Wildlife, would have preferred an official citation, but we took what we got because we never saw hide nor hair of that gray pickup again."

"Let's give it up with a warm welcome for a good friend of mine, Burt Cosgrove, who owns Varmint Vigilantes, a Central Florida business that specializes in critter control, big critter control, as in alligators, bears, and those real unwelcome visitors, the exotics. Burt will tell you about a true happening involving Delbert and one of those mean, mean exotic critters.

Burly Burt Cosgrove strode to the microphone chewing on a toothpick. He wasn't a cocky guy, simply a confident fellow with no elaborate airs or strict manners, for that matter. All business in battling nuisance, unwanted animals found in the wrong places, was his stock in trade.

"Nice to be here today, helping to salute that main man of our Florida backcountry, Delbert Turner. Yes, like others who have talked to us today, and I'm sure those coming up behind me, I had a real eye-opener about Delbert's vast talents years ago when we chased down a big, nasty Nile monitor lizard released near here close to the St. Johns River. Now, all of you, being good, ole' timey Florida stock, know what exotic animals are, right? The same label is used for plants. Exotic means non-native, referring to animals and plants brought here out of their own element. In recent years, there has been huge traffic in these animals throughout Florida, and many of them are nasty mean and prey on our own native animals. I'm talking about Burmese pythons, Nile monitor lizards, Gambian rats, lionfish added to aquariums. On and on.

"Many folks with a good bit of pocket change and big, wheelbarrow-carrying egos, buy these exotics when they are small and cute, and then later on, when they grow big and hard to manage, they throw them away on the sly, looking the other way like they don't give a hoot about anybody else's future with these varmints. Being let loose in the wild, these nasty varmints keep me hopping and making a living.

"Well, some joker released a Nile monitor lizard, a mean-looking ole boy he proved to be, over near I-95, probably between Mims and Geneva. No doubt they drove that big, mean critter up from the Miami area, dropping it far away so it wouldn't ever

come back to eat his secret owner out of house and home. Delbert's reputation was known far and wide, and he was included in our hunt. I expected a pretty fair country helper, given his reputation, but I wasn't prepared for how really super he was.

"Delbert stayed out longer and worked harder than anyone on our search team. Anyone! Once he learned the habits of the Nile monitor lizard, which took only one day with his animal skills, he was on the hunt, big time. When Delbert heard how they can be drawn in by strong smell, he volunteered, the only volunteer, to allow himself to be smeared with squid guts and fish guts, making himself a human banquet target for the lizard that had been spotted in a certain area by hikers. Here Delbert was, wading in water, smelling like a septic tank, trying to lure in a wild animal. It worked. After three long days in this big area out there, Delbert attracted the lizard close enough for my men to get a good shot at it. We had to kill it. We tried and found no zoo interest, calling all across the country after we learned of the lizard loose in our backyard. Delbert turned the trick with bravery and guts of his own. Can't begin to say enough about Delbert Turner. Shucks, his name is already on this building we're in today."

Twice during the long, but highly compelling parade of presenters, Dan announced short intermissions for refreshment of drinks and necessary comfort visits, but folks were back in their seats promptly, eager to hear more, showing absolutely no signals of flagging interest or numbing boredom.

The list of presenters continued at the microphone, and the two bands, trading gig time, kept up their musical excitement to the delight of everyone.

Hearing about Delbert's vast skills from Dan, Lois Spense, the owner of a popular pontoon boat ecotourism business on her beloved Ocklawaha River, glowed with praise about Delbert's expert help in clearing deadfall limbs and drooping understory, feats allowing her to continue operating to the delight of her river customers.

Hugh Cameron, the owner of an emu farm in Brevard County, wagged his head in disbelief when he told the hushed audience about the day Delbert captured an escaped, disoriented emu in ten minutes after the giant bird had foiled capture for five hours with eight of his farmhands engaged in unsuccessful, bungling pursuit.

Fire rangers bragged about Delbert's worth during ravaging forest fires plaguing east-central Florida on numerous occasions. George Mason told about their recent grasshopper sparrow success. And, Dan, late in the marvelous lunch program, kept repeating that the event was the toast of all toasts he had ever attended.

It was almost two o'clock, three hours after folks had begun to arrive, before the attentive audience was finally treated to Delbert himself standing up and walking to the microphone to receive the well-deserved plaudits from everyone celebrating the triumphs of his life.

Cameras whirred and flashbulbs lit the room, popping and blinding momentarily. The two bands played together, plucking and strumming at a fever pitch. It was a controlled but wild scene. Not one person had darkened any side door, with an early exit. Everyone had stayed to the end.

Delbert stood silently for a moment at the microphone, trying to smile with appreciation. He managed to accomplish his intent, somehow beating away the minions of shyness and humility.

"Awful nice you treasure of great folks a-comin' out this way. I were plum surprised. All I ever done ifin it was good like you done said, I done because it needed doin'."

The best applause was saved for last. Folks cried. Folks cheered. And, Delbert wished to God he was alone in a canoe paddling somewhere on the Wahaweechee River.

And thusly, ends the saga of Delbert Turner.

He still lives, a bright, shining and everlasting beacon for all of us.

Summon All Heroes is the fourth book in the very popular Delbert Turner, Florida's "Man of the Woods" series.

The first three are:

The Morning of Joy (2005)
The Cry of the Hawk (2008)
Memory Evergreen (2010)

All these books are still available in print.

Kindly write:

> SABAL PALM PRESS
> Post Office Box 756
> Goldenrod, Florida 32733

Or

Call the Author:

> ED L'HEUREUX
> 407/696-7222
> 407/619-3103 (cell)

to order.

Thank you so much for being our book customer. You are appreciated. Truly!

ABOUT THE AUTHOR

Born in upstate New York, Mr. L'Heureux grew up in Central Florida, and has spent his adult life there. He attended schools in Winter Park, Florida; graduated from Stetson University; and also studied law at the University of Florida and Stetson University.

Over the past forty-four years, he has pursued careers in the securities industries, in commercial real estate, and in the field of insurance. He recently retired, 2002, from the insurance business, ending a twenty-six year career.

Writing has always been a favorite pastime, with great emphasis, avocationally, placed with this endeavor in recent years. After placing a number of magazine feature articles, Mr. L'Heureux published his first collection of short stories, *The Dollar Collar,* in 1986. His second collection of short stories, *The Clay of Vases,* followed in 1988. *You Can't Sink a Rainbow,* his first novel, arrived in 1995.

Another collection of short stories, *A Table Set for Guests,* appeared in 1998. His second novel, *To Lullaby a Dragon,* was published in 2000. And, another collection of short stories, *Tunes Above the Noise,* was released in 2001. His third novel *The Morning of Joy,* a huge success, drew praise in 2005 and it was followed by a sequel, *The Cry of the Hawk*, in 2008, and a third book, *Memory Evergreen*, completing a trilogy, was published in 2010.

The five books in his *Florida Conversations* series (2002, 2003, 2004, 2007, 2012), were his most popular books ever.

He is editor/owner of *The Sabal Palm Review,* a literary magazine designed to showcase the work of emerging Florida poets and writers. Mr. L'Heureux teaches and lectures throughout Florida.

A widower, he lives in Winter Springs, Florida, with his wonderful maltese dog, Bogie.